KATE ALLEN

Fear of Flying

For my husband,
who reminds me every day why life is worth living.

Chapter 1

There are two competing impulses in her mind right now. The first is to run. To where, she's not sure. The second, and stronger, impulse is to scream. Instead, she finds herself frozen to the seat.

"Are you okay?"

Liv pries her fingers from the laptop keyboard and manages to move her head to face the man in the seat beside her. Somehow she contains the reflex to vomit when her eyes catch sight of the window behind him. She nods vaguely, only then able to focus on his face.

He must find her expression comical. She can tell from the slight curl of his lips and the playful light in his brown eyes as they survey her trembling fingers. He's gone to the trouble of lowering the headphones he's been wearing since they boarded. Her ears hone in on the faint dull thud of the bass still blaring. "Nervous flyer?" he asks.

The clouds shift across the window behind him and she looks back at the laptop, gripping both armrests. The words in the unsent email to the college student affairs office blur and seem to vibrate right off the screen. She'd purposely paid extra for the in-flight wi-fi but now regrets overestimating her ability to focus.

"How could you tell?" It's not a joke and it's not delivered as such. It's the only sentence she can manage to flatly speak out loud, queasiness pooling at the base of her throat. "Can you pull down your shade?" If she can't see the clouds, maybe she can pretend she's in a bumpy car. A car that can plummet down to the earth at any moment.

He tilts his head. His cologne is heady with the scent of cedar and ginger. "What?" He glances over his shoulder. "Oh, sorry." The shade clicks with a soft thud as he pulls it down.

"Thank you," she says, finally taking the full breath she's been craving. The nausea ebbs slightly. The turbulence hasn't even come yet, but her body is still frozen from take-off, braced for the next round of trauma. She's convinced herself that maintaining this huddled rigidness will somehow make the jolts to come more bearable.

"It's been pretty smooth so far," the man says in a calm, even tone. "We're probably in for a boring, uneventful flight."

She stares straight ahead. "Yeah?" She can tell what he's trying to do. Normally, she would appreciate it, but today it makes her angry, pushing the fear to the backseat for only a moment.

"So, what's in Amsterdam?" he asks, sliding the headphones from his shoulders and resting them on his lap beside his phone.

She wipes at her eyes, the grit of the smudged mascara rubbing against her fingers. She hadn't even bothered to check a mirror before getting on the plane. "I don't know."

That makes him laugh. "Okay," he says, running a hand across his face, trying to conceal his smile. "Sorry, I was just trying to help, but I get it. You're obviously not in the mood to talk."

Her heart sinks at the thought of going the rest of the flight in tortured silence. "No, that's not - I just - I'm not going to Amsterdam really," she says, finally untangling the words. "It's a layover for me."

He nods. He has a face that could easily belong to a thirty-year-old or someone in her year of college. His skin is absent of wrinkles or lines, other than around the lips, but there's a quiet sophistication uncharacteristic of men her age. Without that, one may even say he has a babyface. "Where's your final destination?"

A bump against the floor sends her hands into a tighter grip on the edge of the armrests, her elbow knocking into the sleeping man in the aisle seat. He doesn't stir. Her stomach drops at the thought of the plane crashing. "Scotland," she croaks. "What about you? Why are you going to Amsterdam?"

He shrugs. "Mostly for the red light district, I guess. But a little bit for the drugs too."

She stares at him out of the corner of her eye.

He catches it and laughs. "That's a joke. Sorry, that was bad."

A small release of tension leaves her body.

"I go back and forth between Boston and Amsterdam for work a lot," he finishes. She rethinks her analysis of his age. He's old enough to have a stable job with international travel involved. He must be well past her age. He's wearing a plain black t-shirt and jeans with minor distressing around the knees, but it's hard to tell if it's fashion or just worn.

"What kind of work?" she asks.

He grins. "Would it help distract you if I made you guess?"

Probably. But something about his manner seems more condescending than helpful, like he's playing with an anxious toddler. Admittedly, she feels like an anxious toddler right now. "DJ?" She means it as a slight, but he smirks and tucks his headphones into the seat pocket in front of him.

"Funny, but no."

She spots the thick class ring on his finger. It's a wonder that she didn't catch it earlier. She's filled with a hollow satisfaction when she makes out the class year. 2014. So he was upwards of 27, at least. "Engineer," she says firmly.

He glances down at his finger. "That's pretty presumptive. Not everyone who graduates from M.I.T. is an engineer."

This is true. But almost all the successful graduates are. Her own parents majored in Philosophy and Anthropology at M.I.T. and died with barely a penny to their names.

"But, I am," he says. "I'm an electrical engineer at an energy company."

She nods, a little disappointed that she no longer has a viable distraction.

"So what's going on in Scotland?" he asks after a pause.

That's the question she's been dreading. "Just a trip."

He glances at her laptop, the draft of an email requesting further deferment from the registrar still open. She doubts he can make out the words on the dimmed screen, but shuts it all the same. She can't finish it right now anyway.

She ventures to look around the plane for the first time in a while and can see the flight attendant with a cart only a few rows away. "So, are you from Boston or you were only there for college?"

The man picks up his phone and then flips it over onto the open tray in front of him. "I'm from there - well, Winchester. You?"

She nods. "Somerville."

The flight attendant is upon them now. He smiles at the sleeping man in the aisle seat and then turns to her. "Drink or snack, miss?" His accent is vaguely European. She assumes it's Dutch.

"Vodka soda, please," her voice overlaps with his end of the question. She's been waiting for this moment since boarding. Even though her 21st birthday was only weeks ago, she's spent the entire time almost perpetually in stages of drunkenness. The gap in time between now and her last drink in the terminal Applebee's has caused a throbbing headache to form behind her eyes.

"Any snacks?" the attendant asks quietly over Aisle Seat before stooping for the lower shelf on his cart and pulling the bottle of vodka.

She shakes her head.

The attendant hands her the drink and looks over at Window Seat. "Sir?"

Window Seat gestures to her clear plastic cup. "I'll take the same and two waters, please." Somehow he already has his credit card ready and passes it to the flight attendant swiftly before she realizes what's happening. She didn't think through the cost of alcohol on the plane. He replaces his card in his leather wallet and takes a sip of vodka. Window Seat places one bottle of water on her tray. "I have a feeling you're going to need this," he says, with a smile. She likes his smile, the way a dimple appears at the edge of his cheek when his lips curl.

"Thank you." Her tone is a little warmer now that she's taken a few gulps of the drink in front of her. She can almost feel the anxiety beginning to release its chemical grip on her brain as the alcohol renews her numbness. That feeling, that brief release of everything is what she's been chasing in the past few weeks. But each time a higher dosage is required.

Window Seat clears his throat and sets his cup down. "As an engineer, I feel like I have some kind of civic duty to let you know air travel is completely safe."

She's heard it all and read it all before. She hates when people say this. "Until it isn't." She means to say it only to herself, but it comes out through her lips anyway. She immediately regrets speaking it, for her own sake. Now, she's shattered her own illusion of safety that she's been struggling to construct. "I mean, I know that, but it's like my body doesn't," she continues after a moment.

"Some say that alcohol only makes it worse."

She can't imagine that's true when it makes everything else so much better.

"How many have you had already?"

It would be an intrusive question if she wasn't certain he can smell the previous drinks on her breath. "A few." She's ashamed to admit the actual total to this man, stranger that he is. It's 9 p.m. but she's had at least twelve, not counting the one in her hand presently. Not all at once, but since rolling out of bed after another sleepless night and leading up to this goddamn flight. She finishes the vodka in one more long draw. "I've had a rough few weeks." More like months, maybe even years. But the last few weeks were definitely the peak difficulty of her life to this point.

He leans into the window behind him to face her better, their legs almost touching. "Is everything okay now?"

She hesitates, the warmth of old tears threatening to renew behind her eyes. She adjusts in her seat to see him better. What the hell? She'll never see him again, right? "No," she answers honestly. She doesn't have to care about making this uncomfortable. He'll probably sleep the rest of the flight and when they part at the gate in the early morning, this will just be a funny anecdote about how he met a girl on the plane who freaked out and unloaded her drama on him. "My mom died two weeks ago." Ella wasn't her mom. Legally, maybe, but not really. Ella was her aunt and the only mother she'd ever known. Ella was her home and now she's gone. For the average person who grew up in a normal, complete family it's hard to imagine that dynamic. But everyone can understand the impact of losing a mother.

He looks into her eyes. "I'm so sorry." There's something about his steady gaze that's comforting but also makes her want to avert her eyes. His words are unremarkable, but their simplicity is a relief. She's exhausted from the "she's in a better place" and "at least she's not suffering anymore" comments. It's like a prod with a hot iron each time she hears it. She doesn't believe in the sentiment behind those phrases even though she wants to now more than ever.

"Yeah. Thanks," she says.

He takes another sip and cups the drink between his hands. "What was she like?"

"What?" She's taken aback by this question although she's not sure why. Maybe because its sincerity is so unexpected. Why would this man ask something like that? Why does he care?

"Your mom - what was she like?"

The burning starts again behind her eyes. "I don't know." She picks at the skin around her cuticles. It's her disgusting habit. She usually keeps her nails painted as a deterrent, but they've been unvarnished and picked raw since days before the funeral. "She was fun and smart." She laments that her cup is

7

empty. "Crazy smart."

From her periphery, she can see Window Seat watching her.

She shakes her head and rubs at the dampness under her eyes. "That's such a stupid, meaningless thing to say." Ella was indescribable.

"No, it's not," he says quickly. "I only hope people say that about me after I'm gone." He laughs. "But honestly, the best I can hope for at this point is 'he wasn't a total fucking moron.'"

She laughs with him at that. Her laughter continues past his, though. She keeps laughing, not so loud that everyone turns to look, but loud and long enough that Window Seat's expression changes. She laughs until it morphs into a strangled sob. She covers her face with her hands and leans her elbows onto the tray. Her body shudders with each breathtaking, gasping, hiccupping cry from her lips.

His hand is heavy on her shoulder, but in a good way, like one of those weighted vests they put on lap dogs scared of lightning. "Why don't you drink some water?" he suggests softly, so close to her face she can feel his breath rustle through her hair and warm the back of her hand.

His hand lingers as she pulls away from the tray and unscrews the bottle of water. He scrambles for a moment before handing her the two cocktail napkins that came with his drink.

She turns away and furiously wipes at her face until black streaks stop appearing on the napkin. Somehow the man by the aisle still hasn't moved in his seat.

Window Seat squeezes her shoulder lightly and then releases it. Liv's normal instinct would be to pull away but, just like his smile, there's something comforting about the weight of his hand.

She faces him again. "I'm sorry." Her voice is thick now.

He seems unfazed. His eyes are unchanged although now his smile is gone. There's absolutely no trace of it. "No, don't be. It's me - I keep making stupid jokes. That's just my default. Sorry."

She lays the crumbled napkin on the tray. "No, it's not that. I've been such a wreck lately." She drinks from the bottle of water, the cool sensation trickling down her throat. She sets it down and meets his eyes. "Actually, that's why I'm going to Scotland," she says, taking in a shaky breath. "She wanted her ashes to be scattered there." Subconsciously, she glances above their seats at the overhead bin.

He raises his eyebrows at that, following her gaze. "Oh."

She nods with a wry smile.

"Oh," he says again. "So, in a way, your mother is still with us?"

She laughs out loud again, taking another sip of water. "Yes, in a way. Don't worry, I didn't smuggle it on."

"I didn't know that's how it works, you know, um...carrying someone's remains on a plane."

She had carefully chosen an airline that allowed her to bring the ashes in a carry-on. There was no way she would take any chances with checked baggage.

"Why Scotland?"

She leans her head against the headrest and sighs. "That's where her side of the family is from. She grew up there. My grandfather uprooted her and her sister when they were little to come to Boston. He got his Ph.D. at Harvard, and then they just never left." She massages her temple with one hand. "She always wanted to go back someday. They still have some family there."

"You mean *you* still have family there?"

She starts fidgeting with her nails again. "I never thought about it like that. I mean, I don't know any of them. They don't even know I exist."

"That's really nice that you're doing all of this for her," he says. "Especially since you hate flying."

She's almost forgotten they were on a flight. The sudden remembrance makes her stomach sink. "Well, I didn't know I would hate it. This is actually my first time flying," she admits. "Now, I can't believe I have to do this all over again just to get back home."

"It'll be easier the second time," he says, smiling.

She glances down at the display on her phone screen. The entire cabin has gone dark, with a few people huddled under their jackets watching the screens on the back of the seats in front of them. "Aren't you going to try to sleep?" she asks.

Window Seat shakes his head. "No. I'll stay up with you."

Chapter 2

Something shifts beneath her head.

She stirs, her body quickly regaining its usual tension. She feels the warm, souring breath on her cheek as she sits up. Her face grows hot as she meets Window Seat's eyes. He's hunched against the closed window, a slight impression on his shirt from where her head rested just seconds ago.

She decides to sidestep the embarrassment altogether. "Did I fall asleep?" she asks outright, looking around and noticing all the passengers unbuckling their seatbelts.

He nods and smooths his shirt down. "I think that last drink really knocked you out," he says, pulling his headphones from the seat pocket and bringing out a dark backpack from under his seat.

She feels her face around her lips, praying that she didn't drool on him.

Aisle Seat is already on his feet and opening the bin. She hears a metallic thud from above and leaps from her seat, but the belt pushes her back down. "Excuse me," she says, rushing to unfasten the buckle. "Please be careful with the black bag."

Aisle Seat doesn't look at her, but takes his green duffel bag and sits again.

She exchanges a look with Window Seat.

He rolls his eyes at Aisle Seat and then glances overhead again. "Is it heavy?"

It takes her a second to realize he means the ashes. "No, but the container is made out of wood. It could crack."

She waits for everyone to slowly start shuffling down the aisle, weighed down by their purses and bags. Aisle Seat jumps up before the row ahead has a chance to retrieve their items.

Window Seat steps into the aisle behind her and easily reaches above her head into the bin, pulling her bag down and slipping the strap over his shoulder. "Let's go," he says.

"I can carry it," she says over her shoulder to him, but he shakes his head.

"No, it's fine."

She blinks as they disembark, her legs almost collapsing with joy at the solid, unmoving floor of the airport. It's so quiet, with only a few storefronts open. All their fellow travelers move like zombies toward baggage claim.

She and Window Seat walk together silently to a few seats by the gate. "Thank you." She extends her hand for the bag.

She's only now able to truly see Window Seat for the first time in real light, not crouched in the dim corner of the plane. He's not remarkably taller than her and he's thinner than he seemed while seated, but his shoulders are broad, like a swimmer. His face isn't nearly as soft as she'd originally thought. When it's not craned to look at her from an odd angle, his face is stretched over strong, cut cheekbones. "Of course." He hands her the bag and she slides the long strap over her shoulders and across her waist, tugging her backpack on over it. "So how long is your layover?"

"Twelve hours." As she says the words, she silently curses herself for cheaping out on the ticket last-minute. She's not sure if she can handle another flight within the same day.

His eyes grow big. "You're kidding! You're not staying in the airport that whole time, are you?"

She had toyed with the idea of leaving the airport and exploring the city, but now that she's here, she just wants to burrow into the floor and wait for the next flight. "I don't know," she answers honestly.

He beams at her. She can see now that somehow he has some dark stubble creeping along the edges of his mouth and jaw. "You're going to hate yourself if you don't see this city while you're here."

She can't possibly hate herself any more than she does at this exact moment, unwashed, hungover, and covered in sweat from white-knuckling the whole trip. But maybe he has a point. "Okay, what do you recommend?"

The smile grows bigger. "I'll show you around, starting with coffee."

"Aren't you exhausted?"

He shrugs. "I'll rally."

"Do you swear you're not going to kidnap me?"

Somehow the smile grows bigger still. "I promise," he says. "I'll even go one further and promise not to rob you. I mean, now that I know what's in the bag, what's the point?"

She returns his grin although she suspects hers isn't as vibrant or as big as his. "Fair point."

"Let me carry something." He gestures to her bags.

She takes the backpack off with a stretch but hesitates. "You have your own stuff to carry, though."

He accepts the bag. "Don't worry, I have a system." He swings one backpack strap of hers over one shoulder and slides off one from his backpack on the other shoulder. "I just need

13

to go grab my luggage." He points down the hallway and she follows, her head pounding in time with their footsteps.

* * *

It doesn't hit her until they're sitting side-by-side on the train. "I don't even know your name," she says, turning to him abruptly. They'd covered a lot of ground on the plane overnight but had somehow skipped right over the basics.

He looks up from his phone and shoves it in the pocket of his black bomber jacket. "I guess you're right. Collin." He extends his hand to her.

She shakes it. It's still just as warm as it was on the plane. "Liv."

He places his hand over the top of her backpack resting on his lap. "That suits you. Short for Olivia?"

"Yeah. They used to call me Olive when I was a kid, but I graduated to Liv a few years ago."

He nods. "Right. Olive's too cute for you?"

"I just found that too many people name their dogs Olive."

"If it's a popular name for dogs, that means it's adorable." His eyes linger on her. Does he find her adorable?

Does she want him to? What exactly does she want from this stranger? To be desired? The thought troubles her for a few reasons. She's been so lonely, not only since Ella's passing but the year leading up to it. She can't even remember the last time she was with a guy. Well, she can. It was over a year and a half ago with her five-week boyfriend in his dorm after they'd registered for the next semester's classes together. That was before she went back home for winter break and everything changed forever for her and Ella. Before she unceremoniously dumped that boyfriend and dropped out of school.

Suddenly Liv's self-conscious about sitting so close to Collin. She must smell and look disgusting.

He looks fondly at her before glancing out the window. "We're getting out here," he says, standing and repositioning her bags and his.

The train reels and rocks to a stop. She follows him out onto the platform, a gust of frigid air refreshing her after the long flight. Spring is colder here than she expected. The canal runs nearby behind narrow redbrick buildings and a bridge lined with bicycles locked and crowded along the railing.

Collin points to one of the buildings closest to them. "Do you mind if I run up and put my suitcase down real quick?"

"Oh." She looks up at the black, iron railing of the stairs leading to the door of the quaint building. "Is this your place?"

"Yeah, my company owns one of the units so we can stay here whenever we travel." He readjusts her backpack on his shoulder. "Do you want me to put one of your bags up there while we walk around?"

Her thoughts are still muddled from the previous night, but she's able to think enough to open her backpack and extract her passport and wallet and shove them into the black bag beside the wooden cylinder containing Ella's ashes. When she zips it up she realizes Collin is deliberately looking away from her. She gets the feeling that he's trying very hard to not seem pushy or creepy. "I'll bring this up with you," she says. From the look of the building, she figures she can easily scream from the doorway for help if she sees shriveled heads dangling from the ceiling in Collin's apartment.

She hangs back behind him as he walks up the steps and in through the front door. He nods to a blonde woman who calls

15

out a greeting to him from the clean, solid white desk in the lobby. They continue on to the elevators.

Collin types something on his phone after hitting a button. "Sorry, I promise I'm putting this away," he says before tucking it into his jacket pocket again. "They're not expecting me in the office until Monday, but I keep getting emails."

It's Thursday. "Why did you come so early?"

The metal doors slide open on the fourth floor. "Whenever they send one of us out here, they make us come out a couple of days ahead to 'acclimate.'" He makes air quotes with his free hand before digging for his keys.

He unlocks the door and Liv rigidly hangs back in the hallway until he turns the lights on inside before stepping in behind him. The decor is all white and shades of beige with accents of exposed red brick on various walls throughout the open apartment. It's light and airy, sunlight streaming in from full-paned windows.

Collin rolls his suitcase beside the slate gray sofa and she sets her backpack beside it.

"This is nice," she says, leaning forward and glancing into the kitchen. The top shelf by the fridge is lined with various types of alcohol, mostly vodka by the looks of it.

He shrugs. "It's fine, I guess. Better than staying in a hotel."

The apartment is devoid of all personality. She imagines it must be difficult for anyone to feel at home there among the fake plants and generic abstract art framed on the walls.

He turns to her. "So...Amsterdam. Are you ready for it?"

"Ready for what exactly?"

"To see the city. Let's go!"

He gestures for her to follow him before heading out the door. Excitement builds in Liv as they retrace their steps to exit the building. Once on the street amongst quiet but busy strangers, Collin's path is resolute.

As she follows him, her feet scrambling to keep up with his long strides, she notices all the beautiful, but stoic people walking in a hurry or speeding on the road in colorful, antique bicycles as they approach the canal. The same bicycles number in the hundreds in parking garages beside the bridge. "Wow, people really like to bike here, don't they?"

Collin laughs. "Yes, generally speaking, I'd say they do. So naturally, I figured we'd rent a couple of bikes and see the city."

Her heart sinks. "Oh, well...what about we do that canal tour thing instead?"

"We were just stuck on a plane for eight hours straight. I thought it'd be nice to move a little. What do you say?"

"Um..."

"And the rentals are right by the bridge."

She turns her head. So they are. All those shiny, pristine white bicycles locked along the river. She glanced back at Collin, his excited expression holding her back from telling him the truth. "Yeah, okay."

She doesn't know how to ride a bike. She never learned. It was just another thing that slipped through the cracks when raised under unconventional circumstances. She'd never asked Grandpa or Ella to teach her. Not because they would have been angry or put-out, but out of guilt. Every time she saw her friends with something she lacked—like a new puppy or riding a bike, she was plagued with a deep sense of dread. She knew neither Ella or her grandfather had chosen to raise her. Because of this feeling, she tried to occupy less space in their lives somehow.

But they wouldn't let her get away with it for too long. They would go out of their way to surprise her every birthday and spend hours to help her with homework at the expense of piling dishes, taking half-days off from work to see her kindergarten plays and graduations, even when those few hours would have helped reduce the stack of bills. Although they tried so hard to build an illusion that Liv was wanting for no experience, occasionally they missed something. And when they did, she kept quiet.

"Collin, wait." She's already imagined taking a flip over the handlebars into the murky canal below.

He releases the bike he was about to unlock. "Yeah? Everything okay?"

"So, I actually don't know how to ride a bike." She says it so quickly she hopes he doesn't have enough time to really understand her.

He raises his eyebrows. "Oh...okay. Really? Never?"

"I never had a reason to. Anyway, can we take the boat or whatever?"

He bites his lower lip. "If we take the boat we won't be able to get to this overlook I wanted to show you. What about if I teach you how?"

Her heart flutters with both excitement and anxiety. That could be very romantic. Or it could end in him laughing at her or getting sideswiped by one of the expert cyclists whizzing by right now. "I don't know..."

"Come on! It could be fun. And it's a crucial life skill."

She rolls her eyes. "Well, that's just not true," she laughs. "I already told you that I've never needed to learn."

"Okay, fine. Then think of it as a kind of souvenir. One that you don't have to wrap in bubble wrap and put in your carry-on." He smiles. "Whenever you want to remember what your first trip to Amsterdam was like, you only have to replay the memory of me teaching you how to ride a bike."

She surveys the sidewalk. It's the middle of the workweek. Why is it so crowded right now? "Alright, fine."

His eyes grow bigger. "Great! You won't regret this!"

"Don't make promises you can't keep."

"Okay. How about this one? The view from the overlook will definitely be worth it!"

* * *

He was right. The city is breathtaking from A'dam Tower when they arrive an hour later.

After much hesitation, Collin had finally convinced Liv to relinquish her grip on the bridge railing. He'd held the bike between the handlebars and walked backward, never once tripping over the uneven sections of the cobblestone sidewalk. He'd smiled the whole time, continuing to hold on until they locked eyes. "You've got this," he'd said. "Are you ready for me to let go? I won't let you fall." Even though she didn't want him to let go, she forced a nod and when he did release his grip, she didn't fall. She even managed to turn around and make it back to a beaming Collin.

"So? Did I keep my promise? The city's gorgeous from here, right?" he asks now, peering through the glass window beside her.

They'd arrived at the lookout just as the sun began its descent behind the city, casting a warm light on the water that the ships sliced into golden ripples. The tall and narrow buildings beyond the water stretch and fade at the tips into the fiery sky. "Yes, it's amazing." This moment is undoubtedly worth the at-times harrowing bike ride. And she's certain Collin was right. She'll replay this memory often.

Chapter 3

"Maybe you should take it easy." Collin's warning comes after she's already downed four shots of Jenever.

This bar near his apartment was their final stop after returning the bike rentals. She sets her glass down and glances around the cozy, dark bar for their server. "I'm fine." The words come out of her mouth delayed and slurred. "What is this again?" She shakes the empty shot glass.

Collin finishes his drink and puts the glass on the table between them. "It's like Dutch gin."

She nods. Here, the cold air rushes in from the canals and through the bar door as a new patron steps in. March here is colder than Boston right now, but the icy breeze doesn't bother her. Rather, she enjoys the feeling of wrapping her wool peacoat tighter over her chest. His deep brown eyes, like chocolate, follow her as she raises two fingers to beckon the bartender, hoping this signal is universal.

"You know, most people here can speak English," Collin says.

The red-haired bartender takes her glass and replaces it smoothly with a tired smile.

"Thank you," she says to him as he walks away. She turns to Collin. "I didn't want to assume." She hadn't really heard many people speaking except for other patrons of the bar. Although the words she did hear were interspersed with familiar English words like 'menu' or 'check.' "Do you know any Dutch?"

He smiles wryly. "Eh...not really any worth mentioning," he says. "I've just picked up a few phrases here and there. And I probably pronounce all of them incorrectly."

"How long have you been coming here?" Other than the quick exchanges during their meandering tour of the city, she's realized she barely knows anything about his life. The night on the plane had almost been exclusively filled with questions and answers about her. She knew he was an engineer, that he had two sisters and one brother, his family was extremely tight-knit, and he was the only one not working in the medical field. His parents were both doctors and his siblings a mix of RNs and physician assistants.

He settles back into his chair. "About six years now?" He rubs at the small shadow of hair beginning to creep up from his jawline. "I've been working for this company since my senior year of college and then after a few years I started splitting my time between here and Boston."

"Which place do you like better?"

His eyes narrow at her but his grin is still apparent. "You're a native Bostonian, right?"

"Yes. Why?"

"You're not going to claw my eyes out if I don't say it's my favorite?"

She laughs, almost spitting the gin from between her lips. "No." It's not a silly assumption on his part. Bostonians can be rabid about their enthusiasm for their city. "No judgment here," she says. "I've been wanting to get out since I was little.

I'm just curious since you've been, you know, out in the world."

"Okay, good. Amsterdam, of course." He takes the new glass of Jenever the bartender places in front of him and sips.

"How dare you! That's sacrilege!" She tries to keep a straight face, but a smile creeps over her lips. "No, I mean, I totally agree." From what she's seen, there are many similarities between the two cities. Both places are littered with relics of their varied histories, which at times is at odds with the modernity of street art and graffiti.

"I think it's beautiful here. Not that Massachusetts isn't."

Boston has a lot of charm, but she prefers Amsterdam too. Maybe it's only because Liv hasn't traveled much and the city is so exciting and lively. Boston is more somber somehow.

She wonders what Scotland must be like. Her grandfather often lamented never making it back, but he always said they would all go together to visit one day. When he was gone, Ella promised she and Liv would make this journey in his honor. Ella had often told tales of her childhood in Scotland with the same sweet and soft gaze that Collin has now as he glances out the window at this city.

"Back home, what are you studying?" He turns his attention back to her, that gentle look remaining as he regards her.

She told him on the plane that she'd taken a year off whenever they found out about Ella's diagnosis. He'd kindly and quietly listened but now she realized he must've been stacking up questions in his mind, reserving them for later.

"I *was* a Communications major," she says. "But I don't know if I'm going to stick with it."

He furrows his brow. "Why not?"

She doesn't really know why she's lost interest, other than the recent perpetual apathy about school and the trajectory of

23

her life in general. "I don't know what I'd do with a degree like that."

"What did you originally want to do with it?"

What a simple, yet profound question. She hasn't dared ask it of herself, but now that it's spoken aloud a quiet yearning stirs in her. "I wanted to be a journalist."

"That's great," he says, his eyes widening.

She had thought so once. But the turmoil of the world had taken its toll on her over the years. Coupled with her own personal tragedies, the largeness of the world's problems was an all-consuming fire that she's already burned her finger on. "Yeah, but not anymore," she says. "Actually, I'm not sure I ever really wanted to be a journalist. I wanted to write books, but I figured a Communications degree would be more marketable than English Literature. Now, I honestly have no idea what I'm doing."

"We've all been there," he says after a moment. "Hell, I'm still not sure if I made the right decision choosing to go into my field."

She looks at him. "What do you mean?"

He downs a gulp of beer. "All throughout high school I wanted to become a professional musician."

"So, why didn't you? What changed?"

He laughs. "Believe me, I tried. I figured if me and my friends could really 'make it,' we could all drop out of college and make it work." He shakes his head. "I was working gigs at night all week, by myself and with the band, and going to school full-time. Eventually, something had to give and it didn't seem like music was really going to pay off." He catches her disheartened expression and quickly adds, "Of course, writing is a more transferable skill than music."

She sighs. "It feels like there's really no point in trying to figure it all out now anyway. There's no one looking over my shoulder anymore to make sure I'm going to make something of myself."

Collin twists his glass in his hands. "Do you have any other family?"

She feels the wind knock out of her. "No." She appreciates that Collin hides his surprise well when she says this. It's rare. Most people she meets find it strange that she has little (and now, no) family. "My mom - Ella - was my last tie to family. Actually, Ella was my aunt," she admits.

He doesn't really react but continues to watch her.

"She adopted me after my parents died when I was little."

"I'm sorry. That must've been hard for you."

Tears form at the lower rim of her eyes. "It was." Truthfully, she can't even remember if it was really that hard for her. She'd never known anything different than living with the vague and tiny fantasies of who her parents were and what could've been their happy little family. "They were in a really bad car accident." They died instantly. Or so Ella maintained until her last breath. Liv never had the courage to check what happened.

"Jesus," Collin says under his breath.

She swirls the beer in her glass. "Ella was only twenty-five when it happened. She put her whole life on hold to raise me with my grandfather." A teardrop finally escapes between her lashes.

Collin reaches his hand past his glass and gently places it on top of her closed fist. She wants to melt into that feeling of comfort.

She wipes at her cheek. "It's a little complicated, so I said she was my mom. I mean, technically, she was. She adopted me, but to me she was...god, I don't know...just Ella." Somehow more and then also not quite a mother.

"She sounds incredible," Collin says.

Liv doesn't want to look up at him right now for fear of the pity she'll find in his eyes. "I swear I don't usually cry this much, especially not in front of strangers." She attempts a small laugh but it sounds more like a yelp. "It's getting pretty late. Do you want to head out?" She says this before she remembers she still has another six hours until her 3 a.m. connecting flight.

He releases her hand and takes a quick gulp of the remnants of his beer. "Yeah, sure."

As they walk back to his apartment, she takes note of his silence and feels guilty. She already confided in him on the plane about Ella's illness and death. Unloading that kind of information on him was too much and then now this.

He opens his mouth in the dark as their path parallels the moonlit canal. "Was she your mother's sister?"

"Yes. Why?"

Her heart thuds faster as he slips his hand into hers as they walk. The movement is so smooth, she's sure he does this often. That thought doesn't make her angry or jealous, it merely lingers for a moment before he answers, "Just curious."

They both had too much to drink and they've both been awake together for over forty-eight hours. Maybe she shouldn't be surprised that he's reached for her hand. She clasps her fingers tighter around his, wishing she could transfer this warmth into her. "I forgot to ask you...what do you play?"

"Hmm?"

"What instrument?"

26

"Ah." He scratches the back of his neck. "Guitar."

"Of course," she playfully knocks her shoulder against his. "You probably played it at all the parties in college, didn't you?"

"No," he laughs. "Those guys are the worst."

"You totally did. It's fine," she says. "If I could play anything, I probably would show off too."

He releases her hand and wraps his arm around her shoulder as they walk. Somehow this feels even better. "How much more time do you have left before your flight?" he asks.

A sudden warmth fills her cheeks. "My flight's at three, so I'll probably go back to the airport."

He frowns. "You didn't plan on finding a place to shower or take a nap between flights?"

"Actually, I did book a spot at a hostel just in case." She'd been so indecisive about whether she intended to check out the city or not and ended up spending the extra $60 to reserve a spot.

He turns to her, his eyes wide with horror. "Absolutely not."

She almost knocks into him, he stopped in the path so abruptly. "Why?"

He resumes walking. "The hostels are all in a very bad part of the city."

Yeah, she noticed that before she booked. Still, she'd chosen the one that seemed the most tourist-centric. "It's fine. I'll grab my bags and head back to the airport early. I can rest there for a bit."

They take the steps up to his building, their pace much slower than when they were first here hours ago. They shuffle into the elevator even more slowly.

"You can crash here for a little while if you want," Collin says, leaning against the elevator panel. She's comfortable

27

with him. She wants to say yes. But how well can you know someone - anyone - after only one day together?

Once she staggers into his apartment she realizes she's drunk. Drunker than the previous night on the plane and her headache is still stuck behind her eyes. The thought of going back to the airport only to wait six more hours makes her heartbeat quicken. "Can I take a shower?" She's suddenly so aware of her two-day-old clothing and smell.

He rubs his eyes and she can now see they're bloodshot. "Yeah, of course." He groans slightly as he lowers onto the sofa and leans back. "There should be clean towels in the cabinet under the sink."

"Thanks." She grabs her backpack and drags it into the compact bathroom, closing the door behind her. She slumps against it and lazily unzips her jeans, tripping out of them before peeling her sweater off from over her head.

In the shower, she rests her forehead against the white tile, letting the hot water trace along her tired body. She watches the water circle the pristine stainless steel drain and pretends that she can tell which droplets are her drunken tears and which are the shower water. She catches a glimpse of herself in the mirror across from the steamy glass stall.

Her ribcage is more visible than a few months ago before she started substituting most meals with liquor. She cringes as the vision of her naked body overlaps with an image in her mind's eye of Ella's frail body near the end. More quiet tears escape until the supply is depleted. Ella would cry too if she could see Liv now. She'd been crushed when Liv took the year off from school to care for her. She would've fallen apart completely if she had seen Liv lay in bed for days at a time, only accepting copious amounts of alcohol and occasional stale pretzels for nourishment. Or maybe she wouldn't cry. Maybe she would be angry with Liv and make a biting and witty remark about her disappointment that would hurt for longer than a slap.

Liv steps out of the shower and wraps herself in a clean, fluffy towel from under the sink. She doesn't have the energy to use the hairdryer and ruffles her hair with another towel before rifling through her backpack and extracting a clean t-shirt and dark jeans. She pulls the green shirt over her damp hair, noticing the way her clothes hang on her body a little too closely.

She stares at herself in the mirror with detached curiosity. In the past year, her body has become almost foreign to her. She's come to see the entire vessel as an instrument of her own destruction, as the reminder of a grim future she's already witnessed. She misses the couple of years of college when it was mostly a tool for dancing, eating, and drinking for fun (not to forget). She misses that time when she was excited about life and what the future would look like after graduation.

She finishes getting dressed and tiptoes out of the bathroom.

Collin is asleep on the sofa, his arms crossed in front of him, his lips slightly parted.

She wants to let him sleep, but she wants something else much more. She wants to be with him right now. She wants to feel close to someone again. Spending time with Collin has awakened an ache in her as suddenly as it disappeared a year ago, like a roaring hunger after waking from a long sleep. She closes the door loudly.

He jolts awake and looks at her. He stands up, gripping the edge of the sofa for support.

"You talk in your sleep," she teases.

He yawns and stretches, the bottom of his shirt raising

slightly to expose the skin above his jeans. "Did I say anything good?"

"Something about the price of a human kidney on the black market, so I think it's best if I leave."

He blinks and then the joke lands in his mind. "Oh, sorry," he laughs. "You weren't supposed to hear that."

She takes a few steps closer to him, making sure he can get a good view of what she looks like outside of her discarded sweater. "Is it okay if I lay down for a bit?"

He doesn't step away from her, his breath growing shallow. "Sure," he says quietly, his eyes drawing a line from her lips to the low neckline of her shirt. "What time is your flight? I can wake you up if you want."

"It's okay, I'll set an alarm." She bends over, pulling her phone from her bag, her shirt dipping further down her collarbone as she does.

"Okay." His breath catches and that sound stirs something deep within her.

Liv straightens, letting the phone drop back into the open bag. She steps over to him again, extending a finger and touching where his shirt sleeve stops at his bicep.

His hand rests on her waist and directs her body toward his. She takes his other hand and places it on top of her chest.

The pressure of his touch grows firmer as he squeezes her closer into him at the hips, kissing her. His mouth is hot and sweet. Even though he didn't have a chance to shower, his thick musky odor isn't unpleasant. It makes her want to breathe him deeper within her.

He's different in bed than the college boys she's been with, not that there have been many. The boys were always so eager and in a single-minded frenzy to have her body and then finishing in seconds. They writhed on top of her, content without any sound or encouragement from her body as if she were a doll.

Collin is intentional. With every touch, her body responds, hungry and aching for more. By the time he finishes, she feels full and tired, not empty like with the boys.

He struggles to catch his breath as he lays beside her, his arm cradling her neck. "What just happened?"

Liv's body quivers, but it's hard to tell if it's from the fatigue, the grief, or some kind of relief. She touches his bare chest, grazing his skin with her fingertips. "We had sex," she says. "A couple of times."

He nods as if he's had an unexpected realization. "I know, but are you sure? The last thing I remember is falling asleep on the couch. What if this was all a dream?"

"That's fine. Maybe it is."

He slips the sheet down until it's down around her knees. She doesn't protest. His free hand becomes busy then, caressing whatever it can reach.

"Don't stop," she tells him. Because when he does, she'll be empty again.

Chapter 4

"Shit!"

Collin opens his eyes, a flash of skin and long, dark hair frantically leaping from the bed beside him. He sings a silent hymn that he didn't close the curtains before they collapsed asleep. He can see her now completely in the sunlight streaming in from the windows. Liv's bare body is backlit as she arches over the bed, feeling on the floor for her clothes.

An ache throbs deep within him. So, it wasn't a dream.

"I missed my flight!" she shouts.

Collin props up on one elbow and looks at the alarm clock on the other side of the room. She has missed it, by four hours.

She slips her shirt over her head and wriggles into her black cotton underwear, still searching for her jeans. "Shit, shit, shit," she mutters, running into the bathroom.

He leans back onto the bed.

She was so present when he touched her last night. So quiet too, her eyes screwed shut and her breath desperate as she pulled him closer.

Her body and skin felt new and different from the other women he'd been with. Much like the way she spoke, there was nothing artificial or manufactured about her reaction or movements. She was really feeling everything. He loved that he could make her move like that just from his touch. That she hugged her knees around his waist to pull him deeper within her. How long had it been for her?

It had been a while for him too. He enjoyed clubbing occasionally and the women he ended up with usually came from there or his frequented bars. But recently, he'd lost interest in going out much. It was too repetitive and all the conversations with the girls there felt scripted and too exhausting to carry on after two beers.

He'd given up on meaningful connections after Jessica. He hadn't abandoned them entirely but was taking a break. Liv fundamentally felt different, smelled different from the girls he'd been with since.

When Liv opens the door to the bathroom and steps out, she's less frantic as she sinks onto the far edge of the bed in defeat. "I guess it doesn't matter," she says, pushing away a few strands of black hair from her face. "I've already missed it, right?"

He absently makes a note of where his shirt and jeans are on the floor beside him. "I think so. It was the 3:20 a.m. flight?"

She nods and then covers her hands with her face.

He sits up and rests a hand on her shoulder. "Hey, it's okay. I'll take you to the airport and we'll figure it out." *We'll* figure it out, huh? He doesn't like the way that pronoun tumbled out from him. This sense of responsibility he felt for her materialized in that moment on the plane, when he saw her red nose and the raw, rubbed skin above her lip and under her eyes.

She glances back at him now. Good, at least she's not crying. "Okay," she says. Her forehead scrunches as she thinks better of it and shakes her head. "I'll call the airline right now." She paces to her backpack and fishes her phone out.

Collin stands, a sudden sharp throbbing in the back of his skull. He always forgot how bad the Jenever hangovers were for him especially as he crept closer to 30. He abandons his clothes where they are on the floor. "I'm going to take a quick shower," he says from the bathroom doorway.

Liv turns and catches a glimpse of him before he can shut the door completely. He sees her embarrassed smile right before it closes. Her expression makes him laugh to himself as he steps into the shower. Even with the water running, he can hear Liv's anxious voice in the other room. By the time he comes out with a towel wrapped around his hips, she's writing on her palm with a blue ballpoint pen she's snagged from the kitchen counter.

"Okay, thank you," she says before hanging up. When she notices Collin combing through his suitcase behind her, she jumps a little.

"What did they say?" he asks, pulling out a clean sweater from his suitcase and slipping it over his head. The fabric roughly grazes the edge of his chin and he realizes he forgot to shave.

She sits on the edge of the bed, pulling one leg underneath her, the other one dangling over the edge. "I booked the earliest flight. It leaves at noon."

He buttons his jeans under the towel before letting it fall. "Perfect," he says. "So you have time for breakfast."

Her face is impossible to read in that moment, but it's a cross between embarrassment and relief. "Yeah."

* * *

With coffee, her eyes are somehow brighter. She doesn't

seem to like the way coffee itself tastes because she orders the sweetest drink in the cafe. It has whipped cream with cinnamon dusted on top. He's almost forgotten how much younger she is than him until this moment. She looks small and childish, cupping the large white mug between her hands.

"I forgot to ask you," he begins. "Where in Scotland are you headed?"

She sets the cup down. "Aberdeen. Have you heard of it?"

"Yes, but I've never been there in particular." He's traveled to Scotland on short weekend trips during his time in Amsterdam, but only to the major cities, Glasgow and Edinburgh. "How long are you staying there?"

She licks some cream from the edge of the mug. "A week," she says.

He takes a sip of his black coffee, hoping the bitterness will ground him to the moment. It doesn't work. He's still thinking about last night and this morning. He's thinking about what else he'd like to see her lick.

Liv takes a long drink and wipes away a lingering smudge of cream from her lip. "I'm sorry about all of this," she says. "I should've gone back to the airport early after all."

He can tell from the slight tug at her lips that she doesn't really feel that way. "No. I mean, I'm sorry you missed your flight, but I'm glad we have some more time to see each other." He's surprised to hear his exact feelings come out in a sentence. Maybe not exactly what he was feeling. No part of him was truly sorry she had missed her flight. He wants her to miss her next flight too.

She smiles. "Me too."

He does feel bad that she probably had to spend extra money to pay for that new flight. "I guess to be on the safe side we should head to the airport now."

She looks down at her phone. "Yeah, I think so."

As they near his apartment again, he sifts through his thoughts from the last night to now. They all rush by so quickly he can barely land on one with any real consideration.

Once they're inside his place, Liv loads her backpack over both shoulders.

This feels like the perfect moment for a clean break. Is that what he wants? There's a strange pressure building in his chest as he watches her unzip the black bag, check the container of ashes with a frown, and then close it.

She walks up to him, seeming small again under the weight of the bags. "Well-"

"Let me have one of those," he says suddenly. "I'll drop you at the airport."

She exhales as he helps the black bag off of her. "Thank you. God, I'm so sorry about all this."

"No worries. We're getting you to Scotland."

They walk quietly from the apartment, Liv's eyes laser-focused on a spot ahead that Collin doesn't see. What is she thinking?

* * *

He knows he'll regret this moment, but he can't bring himself to ask. *It's not a big deal. Say it.*

Liv looks over her shoulder at the security line and then back at him. She's thrown her hair into a topknot, stray, dark threads of hair hanging loose around her forehead.

He wanted to kiss her exposed neck the entire train ride. "Have a good trip," he says instead of what he really wants

36

to.

She grins and leans forward, hugging him from the side only for an instant. "Thanks for everything. I don't know how I would've survived that flight without you."

He recalls her pale face and shaking body on the plane. He can only muster a nod, releasing her hand. "Bye, Liv." *Get her number.* "Maybe we'll run into each other in Boston sometime."

She pushes the hair away from her face and beams at him. "I hope so."

He can see she truly means it from the smile that reflects even brighter in her green eyes.

Just ask her.

The line isn't long at all and she easily goes through in a hurry. He waits to see if she turns around. At the end of the line, as she squeezes back into her boots, she does. She looks over her shoulder briefly and smiles at him one last time, giving a quick, nervous wave—the kind that fades into a stroking of her hair—before disappearing around the corner toward the gates.

Collin continues to stand in place for a few moments longer and then starts back toward the station. He's down the hallway when he looks over his shoulder and sees it. He stops in his tracks. Under a seat, not far from the ticket counter, lays the black duffel with Ella's ashes. He hurries back and scoops up the bag, darting to the security line and peering to the end. Liv's long gone.

"Can I help you?" The agent at the beginning of the line asks, eyeing the bag.

Collin gestures toward the gates. "My friend left one of her bags behind. I need to get it to her."

37

"Boarding pass."

"What?"

"Where is your boarding pass?" The agent repeats impatiently.

"I don't have a flight. I just need to-"

"You can't get in the line without a boarding pass, sir. Please move away from the line."

He knew he should've asked for her number. For this reason, if nothing else. He grips the handle of the bag tighter. What to do? He's basically lived in and out of airports for the past year, but he can't think clearly right now. He can only picture Liv's face crumbling into tears when she realizes the bag is missing.

He bolts to the nearest ticket counter. "Is there any ticket I can get for a flight today," he asks urgently, beating an elderly woman to the counter. "The cheapest one."

The attendant smiles and begins typing on her computer. The typing continues so long he fears he'll go crazy with that repetitive sound.

"Collin?"

He turns to see Liv standing beside him.

"What are you doing?" She glances between him and the attendant with amusement.

He exhales in relief. "Thank god! You left this." He hands her the bag.

Her smile grows bigger. "Thank you. Were you about to buy a ticket so you could give this to me?"

"I didn't have your number and they wouldn't let me in the line without one," he laughs, his heartbeat slowly returning to normal.

"Sir?" The attendant leans over the counter toward Collin. "Do you still need a ticket?"

Chapter 5

Collin scares her a little. Well, not Collin exactly, but rather the idea of him.

She's never really had the impulse to be with a stranger before last night. The two boys before Collin were each her one true loves, or she'd thought so at the time. And with both, she eventually came to understand that she didn't actually love them.

She watches Collin carefully now as he drinks from his white paper coffee cup on the flight. She's scared that he holds some invisible power over her after last night. Like the other boys did. In the past, they had both somehow sensed that her willingness to sleep with them meant she cared too much and used it against her.

Collin notices her staring and flashes a sleepy smile before closing his eyes and leaning his head against the window. "You're thinking about how weird it is that I'm coming with you, right?" he asks without opening his eyes.

Liv studies the line of his jaw. The way the light from the neighboring window casts a shadow along the sharp edge. "No," she says. "I'm thinking how weird it is that I asked you." Begged is more like it. God, she's pathetic. But the relief she felt when she saw Collin standing at the ticket counter had given her the courage to ask for what she wanted.

He laughs, the expression crinkling the sides of his closed eyelids. "Don't beat yourself up. The weirdest thing is that I said yes." He turns and looks at her. The gleam in his eyes reminds her of why she asked. Any trip is better with a friend, especially when it involves such a grim errand. "But, really, it's not weird at all. I'm glad you asked."

She is too. They'd been lucky to get on the same plane together at all. She overheard the ticket price before he paid but he didn't bat an eye at it. He'd handed his card to the attendant at the desk as if in a trance, his expression only flickering once they were in line at the gate. After boarding, she realized with a panic that they wouldn't be able to sit together. Of course. He'd just bought a last-minute ticket.

Collin had noticed the color drain from her face and leaned toward her seatmate in the window and said something in a low voice, gesturing over his shoulder toward her. The old man by the window wrinkled his mustache and peered at Liv before standing and grabbing his leather bag from under the seat. Collin said something to him again as he left and looked at his ticket, disappearing down the aisle without a word. Collin nodded toward her, pleased with himself and settled into the window seat, tapping the seat beside him.

"What did you say to him?" Liv had asked then. From where she sat, she could see the old man sink into the aisle seat a few rows ahead.

"I explained the situation to him," he said to her.

"And what's the situation?"

He laughed then. "He didn't speak English and I only know a few phrases in Dutch."

She waited for more.

"I told him you were sick...and that you've already thrown up today."

Her amusement outweighed her embarrassment. "How is it that you know how to say that?"

He stifled a yawn. "I've seen some pretty rough nights at the club," he said with a smile.

Now, she digs her fingers into the seat as the plane finally takes off. As if he somehow senses this, he reaches for her fist and finds it with his eyes closed. She tries to imagine him in a nightclub in his dark blue sweater and jeans. She can't imagine him dancing. Maybe he drinks and observes. She can picture him leaning across the bar, watching his friends dance, talking with the quiet girls drinking martinis.

She settles back against her seat. Her stomach is queasy and her heart is pounding, but not as erratically when they took off from LaGuardia the other day. She should be too exhausted to be scared right now, but she's still not calm enough to actually fall asleep.

Collin's breath has grown deeper and slower beside her. She looks at him again and her chest feels full. His face is relaxed and softer while he sleeps. She watched him briefly that morning too when she first woke up, before it occurred to her that she missed her flight. She'd noticed how peaceful he seemed. Even when she slept, tension knotted into her body. She curled up with clenched fists, gritted teeth, and woke up with jaw pain and a headache almost every morning of her life. She almost never felt like her brain crossed over into a dream state, it just stewed and filtered the events of her life over and over again.

She traces her thumb across the back of Collin's hand, clasping it tighter. That perpetual stress cycle has caused her to do some stupid things, but this is perhaps the strangest. Perhaps the least dangerous though. They spent the night together and she woke up with all major organs intact, so her initial distrust has faded to a certain degree. This would be the perfect story that she would've shared with Ella when she got home. A heaviness weighs on her throat. Even though Ella had eventually adopted her, they'd spent her entire life as the fun, young aunt and niece. Liv hadn't felt the need to hide much from her. Almost every stupid thing Liv had done, Ella could counter it with an even crazier story. They'd always been more like sisters than mother and daughter. It's unfathomable that she's gone.

Liv remembers what Collin said the day before about her possible remaining relatives. She's unsure how to feel about this prospect. Between the tragic death of her young mother, Grandpa's unexpected death and his wife's diseased death long before Liv was born, and Ella, she's come to think of her family as cursed. Maybe connecting with the remaining Adair bloodline will only accelerate the effects of this curse and kill her faster. Maybe they're all already dead.

She's thankful she doesn't know as much about the fate of her father's extended family, the Zielinskis. He had cut them off – or the other way around – long before Liv was born and Ella had fought to keep it that way. Liv read articles about kids without parents tracing their family, hunting them down, and reuniting. She's never understood this impulse. Even now that she's completely alone in the world, the idea of digging up a family she doesn't want and then being tied to them forever frightens her. She trusts what she's heard about her father – that he was a good man – and so she can only believe that he had a reason for keeping her from his family while he was alive.

Collin's hand loosens over hers as his body relaxes in sleep despite how tightly she squeezes. A bump of turbulence hits the bottom of the plane, sending her heart racing.

Collin stirs beside her. "Hey," he says, straightening in his seat. "Are you okay?"

No, she's terrified. But she nods, biting her lip and laying her head on his shoulder. The plane seems steadier somehow when she's nestled against him.

Chapter 6

Aberdeen is much smaller than the other cities Collin's visited in Scotland. The trip from the airport to the guest house where Liv has a reservation takes a crawling 20-minute drive through empty pastures and quaint houses guarded by fluffy cows. The taxi driver speaks rapidly and with a much curlier Scottish accent than Collin has encountered before. Collin can't make out a word he's said in the last ten minutes. He glances at Liv and she's nodding in affirmation.

"Yes, I can see that," she says.

From the way her head rests against the window that she must be close to collapsing in exhaustion. He was able to catch a few hours of rest on the plane, but he could sense her nervous energy beside him the entire time. As the cab pulls in front of the small, gray house with even grayer eaves, he grabs the strap of her backpack on the floorboards. Once the driver is off, Collin turns to Liv. "Did you really understand what he said?"

She blinks and smiles, adjusting her bag on her hip and walking beside him to the entrance. "Yes, but his accent *was* really thick." She glances around the empty street. By the looks of the streets, almost everything nearby is preparing to close before sunset. The sidewalks are mostly empty at the edge of town. "My grandfather's accent was like that. It never faded."

Of course. She hails from this part of the world. Hell, maybe Collin does too. He's never bothered to try to find out where his ancestors were before coming to America. In the back of his mind, he's always assumed he's mostly Irish, but probably just because he's from Boston. His last name isn't Irish. Or maybe it was one of those covert Irish names, where they took off the "O'" or the "Mac" to blend in better with the English settlers.

He opens the front door of the guest house, a faded, rust color with a small wooden sign hanging above the door-knocker. Liv steps over the threshold and he follows.

An eager woman and man, both in varying stages of graying hair immediately look up from a small desk positioned beside a sweeping staircase. "Hullo, are you staying with us today?" The woman asks cheerily, her eyes moving from Liv to Collin. The man smiles, watching them.

Liv takes a long breath and answers, "Yes, I'm Olivia Adair."

"Of course," the woman says, shuffling through a book behind the counter. "Ms. Adair, one full bed, correct?"

He feels the strangeness of this situation beginning to dawn on him. He's a stranger, an intruder on a deeply personal trip for this emotional girl—that's what she is. Maybe it was a mistake coming here.

The woman grabs her guestbook and sets it in front of Liv, extending a long, feathery pen to her. The whole scene is charming. "Please sign in here."

The room is small, a red and white patterned quilt on the bed and no television in sight. "I didn't want this to be awkward downstairs," Collin begins, watching as Liv sets her bags in one corner of the room. "But I'll go get my own room."

She blinks. "Why? We're both adults and...I mean, it's

45

already happened, so why can't we stay in the same bed?"

"You don't, I don't know, want to be on your own?"

She runs a hand through her hair. "I invited you so that I *wouldn't* be on my own."

"Fair enough."

She walks to the large picture window and pulls the curtains away. "I'm starving. Do you want to get something to eat?"

They hike to the only restaurant still open at the end of the road, adjoined to a pub crowded with ale and singing patrons. He and Liv eat in silence, their eyelids becoming heavier with each bite. Even with the light nap he'd managed on the flight here, he's still exhausted. After their meal, he remembers that he didn't bring any clothes or toiletries. They stop by the big box store on the way to the guesthouse right before it closes.

"I think I'm going to sleep," Liv says suddenly, closing the door to their room when they return. "I'm so tired, I don't think I could even taste that steak."

Collin wants nothing more than to melt into the bed and close his eyes. He glances over at the folded cot in the corner of the room behind the small oak wardrobe.

She catches his gaze and grins. "Let's share the bed," she says, sinking onto one corner and pulling off her shoes. "I'm not going to force myself on you or anything. I'm too tired."

He laughs. "That's not what I'm worried about." He sits down beside her. "I think it's now starting to sink in what a bad idea it was for me to just hop on a plane with you like this."

She frowns. "I'm sorry this is so uncomfortable for you."

"No," he says quickly. "That's not what I meant. It's - this is a really personal thing for you and I feel like I took that away from you by being here."

She looks down at her hands. "You didn't," she says. "I

honestly don't think I could do this on my own. I'm really glad you came with me." She gestures to the bathroom door. "Do you mind if I shower first?"

* * *

He's not sure what prompts it, but after a few hours of deep sleep, he suddenly wakes. For a moment he doesn't remember where he is until he sees the outline of Liv sitting in the dark by the open window. "What are you doing?" he asks hoarsely.

She continues staring out the window. "I couldn't sleep," she says.

He rolls out of the bed with a groan and walks toward her, leaning against the windowsill.

"There are a couple of drunk guys down there singing." She smiles at Collin. "They almost got into a fight, but now they're just singing together."

He glances down at the street and sees two slouching, bearded men, arms around each other's shoulders, belting out loudly as they stagger at a snail's pace. "How long have they been there?"

She points down the street. "They left that pub way down there like 45 minutes ago and they've still only got this far."

He looks at her. "Are you okay? Why can't you sleep?"

She shrugs, pulling her knees to her chest in the chair and winding her arms around them. "Jetlag, I guess?" Her eyes are still red and swollen. He wonders if she's been crying while he was asleep or if it's from the day before. "Or...I don't know. There's too much on my mind."

"Like what?" He prods, concealing a yawn by pressing the back of his hand against his mouth.

"What's your family like?" she asks, tightening her grip around her folded legs.

He sits on the ledge, facing her. "Um, I don't know," he says. "I have one brother and one sister. I told you about them earlier. I'm the middle child."

She smiles. "I always wanted a sister."

He shrugs. "They're okay," he says wryly. "Do you have any siblings?"

"If I did—well, if I had anyone left—I wouldn't be doing this on my own." She releases her legs and lets her head fall back onto the seat. "So you're a middle child? Hmm."

He laughs. "Why?"

"You don't seem like a middle child," she says, meeting his eyes. "Do I act like an only child?"

He raises his palms in the air. "I have no idea. What are only children like?"

"Selfish. That's what everyone says."

He shakes his head. "No, you're not selfish."

She surveys him. "You act like the oldest."

"I don't know what that means."

She settles back in her seat. "I think they're reliable." She shakes her head. "I wouldn't know, but that's what I imagine."

He studies her in the dark. "Then, thanks I guess." He looks out the window. The singing has stopped and the men are nowhere to be seen. "Come on. You should try to get some sleep." He extends his hand to her.

She half-heartedly takes it and pulls herself off the chair. She sinks under the covers and faces him as he slides in beside her, careful to keep his distance. "Goodnight," she says, closing her eyes. Her black hair is painted a deep, electric blue from the glow of the streetlights. He wants to touch it.

"Goodnight."

Chapter 7

The next day, Liv is remarkably quiet. She pushes the scraps of her poached eggs around her plate. She barely takes two sips of her creamy coffee. Collin woke up hours before she did. He was worried at first, but let her sleep. It's well past noon by the time Liv wakes and they make it out the door.

The way she moves through the afternoon is as if she hasn't actually woken up. He follows her like a shadow as she drifts around the city. "I'm sure this is it," she says after hours of walking with only a few breaks, suddenly stopping in front of a sleek, gray apartment building, towering overhead.

"What?" He watches as a couple exits through the glass doors of the building.

Her eyebrows knit together. "This is where the house was."

It takes him a moment to understand. "The house your family used to live in?"

Her eyes search around the hideous, modern building. "Yes," she says. "This was the street. At this corner. Ella said there was a garden behind the house." She takes a deep breath.

"It's been a long time, right? The owners probably sold it to a developer or something."

"Yeah, I guess so." She looks up at him. It's the first time she's really acknowledged him since breakfast. Her eyes aren't bloodshot anymore, making the emerald color of her irises brighter. "Now, I don't know where to go...with Ella." She clutches the black bag closer to her hip. "What should I do? There's no way I'm going to leave her in front of *this*." She scowls at the apartment complex before scratching a hand through her hair.

"What about a park?" Collin offers cautiously. "Or the beach?"

She stares at him and then gives a sharp, little nod. "The beach. Yes."

"You really have no interest in connecting with your family here?" he finally asks after they resume their trek in silence. Since he first mentioned it to her, he wondered at her reaction. If she was truly alone, why wouldn't she want to find her family?

"I told you. I don't even know if any of them are still living," she says. "There hasn't been any communication with them in decades."

He catches the first glimpse of the beach coming into view. As they reach the sand, his eyes immediately dart to the huge grey, rectangular rocks here and there. "What are these?"

Liv taps one of them. "Oh yeah. Ella told me about this." She slings the strap of the bag over her shoulder. "This is granite. Isn't that crazy? They just have all these naturally formed granite slabs laying around," she says, glancing along the beach. "It's called the Granite City." Her smile is sad, marked by a gentle decrease in the curve of her lips. Her eyes lock onto the sunset. "There. It's perfect."

He follows her gaze to a cluster of rocks leading into the sea, waves crashing upon it. He hangs back as she strides toward the rocks and climbs onto them. He watches from shore as she walks to the very last one and sinks on top of one of the granite slabs, her back turned to him. He paces the waterline, daring to glance at Liv every now and then as the sun draws closer to the ocean. He sits on the sand, looking on as she buries her face into her knees on the rock.

After the sun has completely disappeared from the sky, he continues to wait until finally she crawls to her feet with the deflated duffel bag and holding the small wooden box. He meets her at the edge of the rocks and puts his hands on her waist, lowering her back onto the sand.

Even in the dark he can see her swollen eyes and hear her sniffling over the sound of crashing waves. They walk in silence into the town, tracing their way past the townhouses and ancient university buildings.

She abruptly slips her hand in his. "Want to go get a drink?"

* * *

"So, why the beach?"

Liv stares down at her frosty glass. "What?"

Collin settles into his side of the booth, glancing around the pub before turning back to her. "Did Ella like the beach?"

She nods, unable to find the energy to provide further affirmation. But she feels guilty when she notices Collin's expression, waiting for more. "Yeah, I guess." The truth was it was almost impossible to keep Ella away from the beach. Anytime the weather permitted it, she would pack up supplies and food for a day at Castle Island. Unfortunately, when she was at her sickest it happened to be winter. But even in the cold, bone-breaking Boston winter, Ella bundled up and insisted on sitting at the beach, reading and painting for hours since the water was too cold for a dip. "Thanks for suggesting that—about the beach," she says. "I panicked when I couldn't find their old house. I couldn't think straight. I was counting on the house being there...I don't know why. I mean, it's been 30-something years."

Collin nods, taking a sip of his ale. He's been oddly quiet the entire day. Out of it as she had been, Liv had noticed the way he'd cautiously observed her all day. She'd hated it. His hesitancy reminded her of their unfamiliarity with each other. She feels a strong, inexplicable kindredness with him and resents the shattering of the illusion, if only for a moment.

"Do you ever wonder what's the point?"

Somehow he must know exactly what she means by this. He sets his glass down and frowns. "Sometimes, I guess."

She's sure he doesn't. From what she's gleaned of his life story, she can't imagine this guy ever even harboring a singular dark thought. "And?"

"And what?"

"When you think that, what have you concluded? Why bother going through all of this when it's just...too much?" There's no answer that will satisfy her, but she's curious.

"I wish I had an answer." He sighs. "I think we have to just go through it to get to the best parts of life. Usually, when I feel that way, I spend so many hours or days or whatever looking for a reason and then forget about it the next time something truly beautiful happens."

She almost wants to laugh at his earnestness. "Like what?"

He glances down. "Well, like meeting you. And being here with you." He gives her a smile and grasps his mug again. "You just have to wait for the beautiful."

"That's a nice thought, but I can't really imagine that you've had any real problems in life. I mean, you have a great job and you get to travel and live it up in Amsterdam every couple of months."

"I'm also a failed musician, remember?" He pauses to take a long draw of his beer, his eyes glassy. "And I don't have the best relationship track record." He hangs his head. "To be honest, I'm actually coming off of a really, *really* bad one."

Liv says nothing, opting instead to nurse her drink, thankful that it's dulled her brain function a sufficient amount so as to not run wild with this new information. "Oh. I'm sorry."

"Don't be. That's only to say I've been going through my own shit recently. My life's not perfect or anything. Not even close."

Chapter 8

By the time they tiptoe up to their room in the guesthouse, Liv's sobering up already.

Collin's cheeks redden as he sits beside her on the edge of the bed. "How are you?" he slurs, brushing a piece of hair away from her face and tucking it behind her ear. He drank more tonight than in Amsterdam. She wonders if this experience is stressing him out more than he's letting on.

"I'm...okay." She actually means it, but she knows she won't be okay much longer. She wants to say so many things to him. She wants to thank him for being with her during one of the hardest days of her life. Instead, she leans forward and rests her head on his shoulder. She breathes him in, his scent somehow sweeter here than the previous night. "Why did you come?"

"Hmm?"

"Why are you here with me right now?"

He exhales.

His hand lifts her chin up. He pauses, cradling her face in front of his. She can smell the beer on his breath. He kisses her before abruptly pulling away and furrowing his brow, wiping away the tears that have appeared on her cheeks with his finger. "Liv?"

Her lips find his, her hands searching for somewhere to

anchor on his body, landing at the waistband of his jeans.

His hands are hot against her skin.

She wants to be within her body. Not in her head and not in her heart. She wants to lose herself here, with Collin. Pressing further into him, she fumbles with the buttons on his jeans.

He pulls away and touches her hair gently. "I-what are you doing?" His eyes sharpen focus on her face.

There's a lump forming in her throat. "I'm sorry," she says in a low voice. "I thought...never mind." Of course, he doesn't want her. She's a disaster. She's been nothing but a crying mess since their first encounter. Besides, he's already had her. Once was enough.

He places his hand on hers.

"You don't want me." It's not a question. It's a statement.

He furrows his brow. "Liv, come on," he groans. "Of course I do." His thumb lightly traces the back of her hand and he leans toward her, resting his head on her hair.

"Then what's wrong?" She can feel his pulse quickening under her fingers on his wrist.

"I feel like today hasn't been the best day for you," he says, his voice measured and low. "And I don't want you to hate me in the morning."

"I want to do this." No, she *needs* to. She can feel the emptiness creeping in. But more than that, she needs Collin and to feel closer to him again. "I won't hate you." She lays back on the checked quilt, taking his arms and tugging them gently toward her.

His gaze softens and he lets his hands rest where she placed them on either side of her. She likes the weight of his body on hers, the heat of his breath rustling through her hair. As they kiss, Liv's hands slip under his t-shirt. When they break away for a moment, Collin slips it off over his head. She unbuttons his pants, the cold metal of his belt buckle licking her fingers before she sheds her sweater and pants.

He stoops to her bare stomach and, with his lips, grazes along her skin to her neck. She shivers as his fingers crawl up her inner thigh. With their bodies intertwined, she feels aware of herself in a way that she hasn't in a long time. In this moment, she is a body. Just a body. An empty vessel made to contain this yearning and all of Collin within her.

Her heart races, her skin burning and tense with pleasure when he's inside her until they fall apart, spent and crumbling like sand.

Afterward, they lay in silence on the tangled mess of sheets. The moments drag on and she wonders if he's fallen asleep.

Collin turns onto his side and faces her. "Liv?"

She stares up at the deep red ceiling. "Yeah?"

"What are you thinking?"

"I don't know." For now, she's content to exist without a concrete thought, with only the pleasant ache within her body. She wants to hold onto that feeling without thinking again, or at least for a while. She meets his eyes. "I'm glad you're here."

He reaches out and strokes her face and then slides an arm around her shoulder, pulling her into his chest.

They stay silent and she's rocked asleep by the rise and fall of his chest.

Chapter 9

A pit formed in his stomach this morning.

Now that the weekend has come to an end, the time has come for him to leave her. This realization makes him sick all day. He can barely enjoy his food. Even though Liv's smiling and talking across from him, he can't eat. He's going to miss that smile.

As they take one last walk around the city, he thinks about how he almost *did* miss this entirely. He thinks about chance and coincidence as he follows her into a cramped and stale bookshop formed around an even narrower spiraling staircase for three floors. He doesn't know if he believes in chance, but when she turns to him and beams, he knows he must. Why else would he have come with her?

"Since you have a four-hour flight ahead," she says. "Let me find a book for you. And you have to read it."

"Okay," he grins. He's never been much of a fiction reader and he has a feeling that fiction is all Liv reads. But he promises himself that he will read whatever she gives him. He makes note of the curves of her lips, the gentle stretch in her neck as she scans the shelves in front of her. He wants to memorize the angles of her profile in this dimly lit corner of the store.

She turns to him when she notices his gaze. "What?"

He memorizes her eyes now. He's only now noticed the subtle flecks of amber in them. "Nothing."

She shakes her head and runs her fingers along the spines on the top shelf. "How do you feel about Murakami?" she asks, pulling a thin volume.

He glances at the worn cover over her shoulder. "Who?"

She taps it with one fingernail. "Haruki Murakami. This is short and it's his first novel."

"I trust you. You're the literature expert, right?"

The rest of that Sunday afternoon passes in a blur. The pit in his gut becomes a black hole as they approach the airport.

Liv stands before him by the entrance, like a gorgeous picture painted against the darkening sky through the window behind her. "I don't know exactly what to say to you," she says carefully. "'Thank you' doesn't seem like enough."

In truth, he doesn't know what to say either. "Liv..." he hesitates. "Take care of yourself."

She leans forward and hugs him and he wraps his arms around her warm, little body. He kisses her and she grows softer in his arms.

The black hole has sucked out everything within him, leaving him only with dread. When he makes it to the end of the security line, he turns to see Liv wave at him from the lobby. He doesn't realize until he sits down at the gate that once again that he forgot to get her number. A sweat instantly breaks over his skin and a sinking coldness replaces the pit. He runs a hand over his face. Maybe there's still hope. He knows her first and last name. He knows she lives in Boston. Yes. There's still a way to reach her somehow.

It isn't until he's on the plane, settling into the corner of his seat by the window that he opens the backpack he purchased in

Aberdeen with the bare necessities and sees the book. The book from Liv. He sighs, remembering his promise, and pulls it out. *Hear the Wind Sing* by Haruki Murakami. He's sure she told him what this book was about but he was too distracted trying to record everything about her in his mind before they parted. He flips open the paperback and his heart revives, beating faster. On the title page, just below the typed script, is a hastily scrawled note in pen.

Thank you, Collin. Meeting you was truly beautiful. Call me when you get back to Boston.
   Liv Adair
   (617) 824-0967
   Livyourlife@gmail.com

March 31

9:08 p.m.

TO: LIVYOURLIFE@GMAIL.COM

FROM: CMITCHELL90@GMAIL.COM

Re: Amsterdam is a State of Mind?

Liv!

You're amazing. I almost sprinted out of the airport after you when I realized that I - once again - didn't get your number. I wanted to call you as soon as I got back to Amsterdam but work kind of took over once I arrived. I figured email might be easier to catch you since you're probably back in the U.S. by now and timezones are a bitch.

I'd really like to see you again when I get back to town. I don't know when that'll be, but hopefully soon. By the way, thanks for the book! It was weird, but really good. I don't think I "get" literature, so I'm going to need you to explain this headache over a drink (or five) later.

-Collin

March 31

9:30 p.m.

TO: LIVYOURLIFE@GMAIL.COM

FROM: CMITCHELL90@GMAIL.COM

Re: Amsterdam is a State of Mind?

Holy shit! This just occurred to me, but did you have another layover in Amsterdam on your way back? If you did, I feel even worse that I didn't reach out sooner.

April 1

2:03 a.m.

TO: CMITCHELL90@GMAIL.COM

FROM: LIVYOURLIFE@GMAIL.COM

Re: re: *Amsterdam is a State of Mind?*

Hey Collin!

It's good to hear from you. My sleep schedule was already pretty messed up before, and there's no telling how bad it'll be when I get back from Scotland, so it's probably a safe bet to call me.

As for the layover, no, I didn't have one. I ended up changing to a flight directly from Edinburgh to NYC on the way back. I wasn't sure I'd have enough nerve to change planes in Amsterdam.

And now I'm sure I did the right thing. This flight has been hell.

I'm arriving in a couple of hours and then I'm taking the bus to Boston.

-Liv

Chapter 10

Her heart seizes when the Uber pulls up to the house. She's nearly half-dead from her voyage by plane, bus, and car, but she's wide awake now that she's been reminded of her previous dread about returning home. The driver brings her bags out of the trunk and hands them to her, giving a small nod and "have a good night" before getting back into his car.

She stands at the edge of the yard, facing the pale blue cottage as the car rumbles down the street. The windows are dark and Ella's sedan is still parked in the driveway, punctuating the fact that she's not inside waiting for Liv's return.

Liv drags her suitcase and backpack to the front door, tears pricking the backs of her eyes as she fishes for the keys in the pocket of her hoodie. She's so tired of crying. The door opens and the hallway stretches in front of her, signs of her frantic packing strewn over the warped hardwood floor. This empty space is nothing like the home Ella and Grandpa had created for her over the years.

After kicking the door closed behind her and locking it, Liv abandons her bags and stumbles to the kitchen, immediately searching for something to dull the growing panic in her chest. She settles on what's left in the vodka bottle beside the fridge. She's only one swig in when her phone buzzes. "Hello?"

"Hey! It's Collin."

A warm feeling creeps up her limbs. It's so good to hear his voice. "Oh. Hi." She grips the neck of the bottle and sinks onto the tile floor.

"I'm sorry. Did I wake you up? I figured you might still be on the bus."

"I actually *just* got home. Literally. Are you telepathic or something?"

"I don't think so, but that would be a welcome surprise," he laughs. "You must be exhausted. Maybe we can talk later?"

She glances at the shadows lurking beyond the kitchen. "No, let's talk now. I don't think I can sleep anyway."

"Ah. Jetlag?"

She sips from the bottle. "Maybe."

"What time is it there? 6 a.m.?"

"Yeah." She rubs her eyes. She wasn't able to sleep on the plane at all. She hadn't realized exactly how much of a comfort Collin had been until she was crammed between her disgruntled seatmates on the way back, her nails almost breaking from gripping the sides of her seat.

"How was the flight?"

She groans. "It was brutal...I can't believe I'm about to tell you this, but I almost threw up on the lady next to me. I also may have screamed when we hit turbulence."

He chuckles on the other end. "Aw, I'm sorry. I was really hoping it would be easier for you going home."

"How do you fly back and forth so easily? You must have some kind of secret to stay sane."

"I honestly don't even think about it. I mean, I know that there's a tiny percent chance that something could happen to the plane, but why dwell on it?"

If she could easily dismiss every worry about the uncertainty of her future, maybe she wouldn't feel so lost. "I wish I could just turn off my fear like that," she mutters. "Must be nice."

"I mean, I try to only focus on what I can change. And I can't do jack-shit about the plane. I actually find that aspect calming. I don't have to be on guard or make a decision." A small clink sounds in the background.

"Are you drinking?"

"Yeah, sparkling water," he says between soft gulps.

"Nothing stronger than that?"

"It's only noon here."

"On a Saturday. It's not like you're on the job or anything." She swirls the bottle gently. "Well, I'm drinking vodka."

"Jesus, Liv! I thought you said you just got home?"

"I did...and the vodka was calling my name."

Collin's silent for a moment. "How are you doing - with everything going on?"

She sighs, hugging her knees to her chest. "Not great. The house is so quiet and empty. I don't know how much longer I can stay here." It sounds ridiculous to speak ill of an inherited mortgage-free house, no matter how creepy and depressing it now seems to her.

"Do you think you'll move?"

"I guess not. I love this house, but it's not the same, you know?"

"Yeah, I do," he says, quietly. "How was the rest of the week in Scotland?"

"Lonely." She answers more honestly than she intended. She wanted to seem worldly and unaffected to Collin, but the truth slipped out. After he'd left Aberdeen on Sunday afternoon, she went back to the bookshop but there was no longer any joy to be found browsing through the books alone. She hadn't realized how much she'd grown to depend on him in such a short amount of time until that moment. "I didn't really end up doing much. I probably could have cut the trip short." If she had, she could've saved some money from the pubs where she'd spent most of her days.

"That's a shame," Collin says. "It's such a beautiful place, but I get it. It was a hard trip."

"Enough about me. How's Amsterdam and work?"

"Amsterdam's great, but the people here are still reeling from the loss of the best novice cyclist they've ever seen."

She scoffs. "Surely, you can't be referring to me. I can't believe I let you talk me into that. I must've looked so ridiculous."

"No, you didn't. You're a natural and you looked great - happy, even."

She scratches at her fingernail with her thumb. She had been happy then. It's almost hard to remember a little less than a week ago how unexpectedly giddy she'd been with Collin in a strange city. That feeling seems like a betrayal of the solemness of her trip when she reflects on it. How could she have truly been happy during such a terrible time? "Yeah, well, I hope you got a good look because I'm never riding a bike again."

When she finally succeeds in directing the conversation back to Collin, he spends a half-hour trying to explain exactly what he does at his job. "Basically, I test the equipment to figure out how we can optimize efficiency," he concludes.

"So, what I'm hearing is that you get paid to play with energy toys?"

He chuckles. "Pretty much."

Liv moves to the sofa as Collin answers her questions about how he got into engineering, crediting his natural determination to figure out how things work. "Okay, but M.I.T.? It's not like you can just end up there on a whim."

"Well, yeah. For a long time, I thought I wanted to become a doctor like my dad, so I worked my ass off in school. When I wanted to pivot to engineering, my grades were already where I wanted them."

She'd always thought of herself as a good student, but her grades didn't really reflect any end goal, any determination. She'd studied because learning was a pleasant distraction. Even when she still wanted to pursue journalism, she took copious notes and pulled all-nighters only out of a hunger to learn, not to get anywhere in particular. "What about the music stuff? I thought that's what you wanted to do."

"It was a dream, but I always planned on pursuing something else in case it didn't work out."

Her eyes begin to flutter shut when Collin asks what kind of job she's looking for. "I'm not really qualified to do anything."

"There are a ton of entry-level jobs that I'm sure you can do," Collin says. "If you could do anything, what would it be?"

"I honestly have no idea. Maybe something with coffee? Or books?"

"I mean long-term."

She tugs an ugly knit throw blanket up to her chin. "I don't really feel like there's a point in making long-term plans at this point."

"What is that supposed to mean?"

She tries to keep her eyes open. "It means, it doesn't really matter what I want, does it? Eventually, I'm going to have to take whatever job comes along to make ends meet."

He sighs. "No need to be so cynical about it. If you have an idea of what you want to do, you might be surprised and find something that's perfect for you." Collin pauses. "Liv?"

She can barely muster enough energy to snap out of shallow sleep. "Hmm? Sorry...I think I'm drifting off."

"Oh! Right, I'll let you sleep."

"Wait," she murmurs, hugging the blanket tighter. "Can you stay on the phone with me until I really fall asleep?" It's such a childish question, almost like she's asking him to check for monsters in her closet. But there are real monsters either in her mind or in this empty house - she's not sure which at this point.

"Yeah, of course." His tone grows softer. "Do you want me to talk?"

"You can or...just stay here."

Collin stays quiet, only the distant, soothing sound of a keyboard clicking occasionally on his end.

By the time she wakes up seven hours later, the afternoon light blasting in through the blinds of the living room, she's not sure how long he remained on the line. But she can't remember the last time she slept so deeply.

April 15

10:05 a.m.

TO: LIVYOURLIFE@GMAIL.COM
FROM: CMITCHELL90@GMAIL.COM
Re: re: Amsterdam is a State of Mind?

Sorry I missed your call the other night. How's the job search going? Have you found anything good yet?

I may know someone hiring. It's at a financial investment firm downtown if you have the stomach for that.

–Collin

April 17

3:35 a.m.

TO: CMITCHELL90@GMAIL.COM
FROM: LIVYOURLIFE@GMAIL.COM
Re: re: Amsterdam is a State of Mind?

Thanks, but I'm not sure I'm qualified for a job like that. I'm applying for some sales and restaurant jobs for now. I think those are the only positions I have a shot at actually getting.

–Liv

April 20

1:30 a.m.

TO: LIVYOURLIFE@GMAIL.COM
FROM: CMITCHELL90@GMAIL.COM
Re: re: Amsterdam is a State of Mind?

Liv,

I'll text you my friend's info so you can find out more about the position. I definitely don't think you're underqualified. It's entry-level and it definitely beats having sales quotas and working on your feet all day.

   –Collin

May 13

4:29 p.m.

TO: LIVYOURLIFE@GMAIL.COM
FROM: CMITCHELL90@GMAIL.COM
Re: Checking In

Hey,

Last night I went back to that bar I took you to when you were here and the bartender asked about you. Apparently his name is Finn. Anyway, now I get one free drink every time I go there, so thanks for being my icebreaker. Usually people here keep to themselves for the most part, so I don't often have these spontaneous conversations with strangers, unless it's another nosey American desperate for interaction.

Finn thought you were my sister and was hoping you'd come around sometime. So, if you ever find yourself back in Amsterdam, I know where you can get a free drink.

Cheers,

Collin

September 24

4:46 p.m.

TO: LIVYOURLIFE@GMAIL.COM

FROM: CMITCHELL90@GMAIL.COM

Re: re: Amsterdam is a State of Mind?

Sorry it's been awhile since our last call. I've only been working, eating, and sleeping it seems like these days.

How are you doing? The fall semester's probably going to start soon, right?

I was hoping to be back in Boston by now, but it sounds like my bosses want to keep me working with the team here until Thanksgiving or Christmas.

If you find yourself getting sick of Boston, you would love Amsterdam in the fall. The only thing I really miss here during autumn is Halloween. The Dutch don't celebrate it. But I was here around the same time last year and I found out that they have a similar tradition, Sint Maarten.

Kids here go door-to-door with homemade lanterns to get candy. So it's basically the same, but there are no costumes involved. And if there are no costumes involved, then what's the point?

Anyway, if I don't make it back to the States by October, please promise me you'll carve a pumpkin for me.

-Collin

October 1

2:51 a.m.

TO: CMITCHELL90@GMAIL.COM

FROM: LIVYOURLIFE@GMAIL.COM

Re: re: Amsterdam is a State of Mind?

Hi Collin,

I think classes started a little while ago…

As for Halloween, I understand your pain. I love Halloween, especially here. It's always been my favorite holiday. I haven't dressed up in years for it, but I think you've inspired me. I'm definitely going to make a jack-o-lantern and wear a costume this time.

-Liv

October 5

3:02 p.m.

TO: LIVYOURLIFE@GMAIL.COM

FROM: CMITCHELL90@GMAIL.COM

Re: re: Amsterdam is a State of Mind?

Halloween's my favorite too. Christmas is…fine. But again, no costumes. Haha

-Collin

October 5

11:09 p.m.

TO: CMITCHELL90@GMAIL.COM

FROM: LIVYOURLIFE@GMAIL.COM

Re: re: Amsterdam is a State of Mind?

Just saw your email.

Are you awake right now? I'll give you a call.

-Liv

October 6

7:00 a.m.

TO: LIVYOURLIFE@GMAIL.COM

FROM: CMITCHELL90@GMAIL.COM

Re: re: Amsterdam is a State of Mind?

Shit! I'm sorry I keep missing your calls! I ended up sleeping in.

I'm calling you tonight.

-Collin

Chapter 11

This time she misses Collin's call.

She hadn't seen his email until she was already out at the secondhand bookstore after yet another sleepless night and going through the motions during her shift at Dunkin' Donuts. She couldn't afford to buy any books until payday next week, but she wanted to kill time away from the house before returning to her marathon of insomnia.

She'd found herself going through this same routine - work, then bookstore - almost every evening now, gradually working her way to different sections of the store each visit. Earlier today, that's where she met Logan. In the classics stacks on the second floor.

"Excuse me," he'd asked with a crooked smile when she turned to face him. "Which one of these would you recommend?" He held up two worn leather-bound covers: *Jane Eyre* and *Wuthering Heights.*

She was still wearing her black polo from work, but her jacket was covering the embroidered company logo. "Oh, I don't work here."

The sandy-haired man laughed, exposing more beautifully straight teeth. She looked away from his face, worried for a moment she'd go blind if she continued to stare at the sun. "I know. You just look like you know what you're doing in this section."

She pointed to the emerald green volume on the right. "I prefer that one." She'd always appreciated the optimism of *Jane Eyre*. She explained why when the man asked her, carefully trying to avoid spoilers. "I mean, they're both classics for a reason, but I like to think *Jane Eyre*'s more believable."

In everything that happened next, it was as if she was sleep-walking. For her, every decision these days was exhausting and the outcomes seemingly meaningless, but Logan made it so easy. The way that he asked for things didn't really leave room for hesitation. She accepted his invitation for a drink because of course she would. She didn't have any other plans, did she? Logan had asked.

And after the drinks, when he pressed her - at first, gently and then harder - against the exterior wall of the cocktail bar and kissed her, it wasn't really a question of whether she wanted to kiss him back. Her mouth merely opened in response to the pressure of his hands and body against her.

Then they went back to his luxury apartment. She was already in the Uber beside him when she realized where they were going. And once they were in his bedroom, there was no hesitation. He knew what he wanted to do to her and what she should do for him.

It felt good to be guided, she'd thought. Besides, if she were going to make an impulsive mistake it could've been with someone worse than this god-like bibliophile.

The entire night, the only real decision Liv makes is to not answer Collin's call.

She stares at the missed call notification on the screen of her phone while Logan's in the shower. She opens the email thread with Collin, types an excuse and then quickly deletes it when the water stops running in the next room over. She shoves the phone into the pocket of her jacket on the floor and gets dressed.

Logan emerges in a towel slung loosely around his waist, his hair still wet. "Where are you going?" He walks toward her so fast that she takes a step back as he bends down and kisses her neck. "Why don't you stay?" His hands are already crawling under her shirt and up her stomach.

And so she does stay, laying for hours with her eyes open, weighed down by Logan's muscled arm around her waist. In the morning, before she leaves, she tells him that she hopes he enjoys the book.

"What book?" he asks, pulling on a creaseless, navy suit jacket over a pristine white button-up shirt. He follows her gaze to the copy of *Jane Eyre* cast haphazardly on the kitchen table. "Oh, it's a gift for my sister. She's graduating with her degree in Literature of all things. She likes collecting old books."

When Liv gets back home, she stares at the missed call notification again.

October 31

10:32 p.m.

TO: LIVYOURLIFE@GMAIL.COM

FROM: CMITCHELL90@GMAIL.COM

Re: re: Amsterdam is a State of Mind?

Well, the time has come. It's Halloween and here I am, not at a bar in my costume, but streaming *Friday the 13th* and *Halloween*.

Did you get to do anything fun?

-Collin

November 1

11:12 a.m.

TO: CMITCHELL90@GMAIL.COM

FROM: LIVYOURLIFE@GMAIL.COM

Re: re: Amsterdam is a State of Mind?

Collin,

I dressed up as Dorothy this year. I know, I know. Not super original, but it was the best one I could find last minute.

This guy I met a couple weeks back asked me out and we ended up at a bar in downtown by the River. Honestly, though, the night you're describing sounds more my speed.

-Liv

November 2

6:03 p.m.

TO: LIVYOURLIFE@GMAIL.COM

FROM: CMITCHELL90@GMAIL.COM

Re: re: *Amsterdam is a State of Mind?*

I didn't know you were seeing someone—congrats

Now, I have a few questions:

Who is this guy?

Was he the Toto to your Dorothy?

-Collin

November 2

1:13 a.m.

TO: CMITCHELL90@GMAIL.COM

FROM: LIVYOURLIFE@GMAIL.COM

Re: re: *Amsterdam is a State of Mind?*

Great, hard-hitting questions. Haha!

His name's Logan. He's a first-year associate at some downtown law firm (no idea which one). We met at the bookstore and we've been (kind of) seeing each other since. He's nice. I think you'd like him.

Oh, and no. He didn't go as Toto. We failed to coordinate and he went as a pirate, I think? It's getting harder to tell what people are dressed as.

-Liv

November 7

4:01 a.m.

TO: LIVYOURLIFE@GMAIL.COM

FROM: CMITCHELL90@GMAIL.COM

Re: re: Amsterdam is a State of Mind?

Liv,

He sounds great. Can't wait to meet him.

-Collin

December 16

3:09 a.m.

TO: LIVYOURLIFE@GMAIL.COM

FROM: CMITCHELL90@GMAIL.COM

Re: re: Amsterdam is a State of Mind?

Okay, so I'm FINALLY coming back to Boston!

I'll be in around the week of Christmas. I have plans with my family from Xmas day to the New Year, but I really want to see you before that if you're free.

My flight's this coming Friday so anytime after that I'm open. Let me know what works for you.

-Collin

Chapter 12

She wants to break up with him.

She knew immediately when she woke up that morning. She can't pinpoint the exact moment when she first realized she despised him - or, rather, despised his grunting and the way his hair flops with each movement - but it's all she can think about when she stares up at him as his body contorts on top of her.

"That was good," Logan says, rolling onto the bed beside her. "Right?"

She looks at the ceiling fan above her, mentally tracing the edges of each static blade with her eyes. She had barely awakened this morning before he was upon her, stroking her hair and then mounting her in one swift motion. She didn't even try to make a sound in objection to it. She still feels the heaviness of his hand on her face from the last time she'd tried.

"Mmmhmm," she mumbles. Any other person on earth would hear this response and inquire further.

But Logan doesn't. He turns on his side to face her and tugs at her waist until her body is pinned against his. "I'm glad I came over last night."

She stiffens under his clammy hands. "What time do you have to be at work?" she asks.

His hand glides down her body. "8:00. You?"

She twists away from under his touch as if to reach for her phone, but she leaves it on the nightstand. "7:00," she says. Truthfully, her shift doesn't begin until 11:30 a.m. Another possible reason for detesting Logan today more than usual enters her thoughts as she slips her gray knit t-shirt over her head. She shrugs his hand from the small of her back and picks up her phone in earnest this time.

There's rustling behind her as Logan sits up. "Do you want to get dinner tonight?"

"Sorry, I have plans," she mumbles, swiping along the screen to view Collin's latest message.

"With who?" his fingers creep along the hem of her shirt.

She drops the phone on the bed and glances over her shoulder. "An old friend's in town and we're going to dinner."

He snorts and lays back on the pillow. "I didn't know you had any friends."

Does she hate him? If not, then something incredibly similar to hatred creeps into her throat as he lounges on her bed, his arms behind his head.

She used to look at him and think he was beautiful. Objectively, he is. But now that she knows him, she sees his anger, not his rower's frame and arms. She sees his entitlement to the world and her body rather than his sun-kissed hair and deep brown eyes. "I have to get ready," she says, clenching her jaw.

He meets her eyes for the first time since she woke up. "Are you angry about something?"

She shrugs. "No. I'm going to be late if I don't shower now."

He sits up and pounces, wrapping his arms around her shoulders and pinning her back against him. She used to like the way he playfully grabbed her. But now she knows this type of action doesn't signal any affection. It's possessive, the way a child clings to his favorite toy before someone takes it away. "Why are you in such a hurry?" he breathes into her ear.

She forces the tension from her muscles, deflating against him. "I'm not. I just don't want to get in trouble," she says flatly. Her boss won't care if she's late. He won't even be in until lunchtime.

Logan's hands have already found their way under her shirt again.

She really does hate him.

* * *

Liv finishes wrapping her hair into a mildly disheveled ponytail right as the doorbell rings. Her heart pounds against her ribcage and she gazes into the mirror one more time. She senses that her face appears gaunter than a few months ago. She regrets putting on a skirt. It's December after all.

She sprints down the hallway to her room and snaps up a pair of once-worn black wool tights and tugs them on. The doorbell doesn't ring again, but she can feel him waiting. She jogs to the front door and unlocks it.

When she opens the door, Collin's lithe body is leaning out away from the doorway, his eyes gliding over the facade of the house. "Oh, hey," he says, taking a step back to the door once he sees her.

"Were you checking out my house?" she laughs.

"Yeah, it's really nice," he peaks over her head inside.

It's not really. It's old and wooden, not stone or brick like the neighbors' homes up the street. But a three-bedroom house, no matter how worn down, isn't anything to be ashamed of, even if there's still shag carpet here and there that Grandpa never ended up getting rid of. "Do you want to come in? I need to grab my bag and coat."

He nods and follows her inside. "You look great," he says with a smile, closing the door behind him. "Even nicer than the house."

She turns to the small table just inside the door, grabbing her purse. "Are you ready?" When she looks at him again, he meets her eyes with a gentle gaze.

"Yes, let's go."

"So, a Prius, huh?" she remarks after buckling her seatbelt in his car. "Don't you work for an energy company?"

He furrows his brow as he pulls out of the driveway. "That's exactly *why* I drive a Prius."

"Yeah, but aren't all energy companies evil and trying to drain the world's non-renewable resources?"

He scoffs. "No. I mean, the company I work for is more lightly sinister than evil."

Liv snickers.

"But seriously, my company does a lot with wind turbines and alternative energy."

"Whatever you say. It's very green of you." She glances out the window. With a few turns, they're on the expressway heading into the city. "So where are we eating?"

"How does Italian sound?"

She nods. "Amazing." It's been a long time since she's gone out to eat and actually had an appetite. The thought of garlic bread almost makes her mouth water.

"It's really good to see you in person again," he says, gazing at her before turning back to the road ahead.

She's been scared - terrified - that all the excitement and

emotion building over emails and phone calls would collapse into nothing when they actually reunited. "Same here." But when she saw him, the eagerness in her swelled. "You just got back today?"

"Yeah, a few hours ago."

The bay comes into view in the distance as they exit beside the Public Market. "You must be exhausted." She notes the fine, thin dark circles under each of his eyes, like smudged charcoal.

"A little," he admits. "I barely had enough time to stop home and get the airplane smell out of my hair." But he took the time to shave. The clothes he chose to wear definitely were not from his suitcase. His dark blue button-up shirt is crisp, not a wrinkle in sight. "But I really wanted to see you. I feel like we have a lot to catch up about." His smile flickers as he says it.

She knows why. Remembering Logan makes her smile die too.

"I figured I'd need to see you before Christmas or we'd probably miss each other all over again."

"That's right," she says. "You said you're going to stay with your family for the holidays?"

"Yeah, we're all road-tripping to Vermont for skiing."

This sentence fills her with longing, jealousy even.

He squeezes the car into a tiny spot on the street, skillfully maneuvering horizontally. As he leads the way up the uneven brick road to *La Emporia*, the restaurant he pointed out through the windshield, he continues to close the distance between them. He leans toward her and then pulls back a few inches. When they reach the entrance, he holds the heavy oak door open for her and then trails behind.

The first notes of live music reach her once she steps into the dim, ambient lighting, catching sight of a mustached, older man in a suit sitting behind the piano in the center of the dining room. A host leads Liv and Collin past an elegant wine rack that scales the vaulted ceiling. Collin edges away from her once more before they reach their destination and sit across from each other, even deeper into the restaurant, away from the piano.

"Wine?" he asks.

She nods and he politely murmurs a Spanish or French word she's unfamiliar with to the waiter.

"You like red, right?" Collin says as the waiter begins his retreat to the kitchen.

"Yes, good memory." To her recollection, they'd only had wine once during their weekend together. The rest of their trip had been all ale and Jenever.

He settles deeper into his seat. "So, now that wine is on the way, how's life treating you Stateside?"

She dogears one end of the thin, parchment menu, creating a crease through the elegant print. "It's been okay." In fact, it's been shit.

"How are your classes? When are you graduating?"

Her heart sinks. He'd asked before about school, but it was usually buried in with a few other questions in his emails so it was easy to sidestep. "I'm not in school right now," she says.

Collin's eyes dart to the waiter as he comes and serves their wine.

Liv gratefully takes her glass and swallows a long sip. It's bitter and coats her tongue, but there's still a sweet note.

"Oh, I thought you were planning to go back," he says once the waiter leaves their side.

There's no malice in his voice, but she can detect the sting of disappointment. She's disappointed too. "I just didn't get all the paperwork submitted on time," she lies, stealing another swig of wine.

He eyes her before taking a big breath. "How's Logan? You guys are still-"

"He's good." She regrets ever mentioning him in her emails to Collin. Maybe she could've somehow manifested Logan out of her life by now if she hadn't written about him. "Are you seeing anyone?"

He shakes his head. "No. But I'm thinking about getting a dog."

Liv smiles, relieved to leave the topics of school and Logan behind. "That's a terrible idea. What are you going to do with it when you leave the country?"

He shrugs. "My parents could watch it maybe. They don't live far from here."

They meander in and out of topics, light and heavy, through garlic bread and shared shrimp scampi and beef bolognese, picking up on their last virtual conversations without any lag. It's not until they've already performed a little dance across the table for the check and Collin sets down his credit card for the waiter that he turns to her seriously. "What are you doing for Christmas?"

She looks down at her hands on the table. "I'm going to stay at home for the day. You know, order Chinese takeout, watch movies."

He frowns at her. "What about Logan? He's not doing anything?"

She sighs. "His family invited me to their annual party on Christmas Eve, so I'm going to that. But I really just want to be alone on Christmas." This isn't entirely true. Logan invited her. His family, she's certain, doesn't want her at the event although he didn't say this explicitly.

She had been the Thanksgiving surprise none of them wanted, dressed in pedestrian threads and quickly outed as an orphan when his mother tried to discern if there was any value in Liv by way of bloodline. Still, Liv ended the night without regretting her attendance. As horrible as those people were to her, they were kinder than most of her own thoughts when she was alone these days.

"How long are you going to be in town?" she asks when they exit the restaurant.

Collin buries his hands in his coat pockets. "I never know for sure, but hopefully for a few months, maybe just a couple of weeks."

Her heart sinks. With the holidays approaching she probably won't get to see him again if he has to leave in a few weeks. Not if he's with his family and if she's still tied to Logan.

"Do you have time for coffee?" he gestures up the street.

She can make out the small wooden sign up ahead in front of her usual bookstore. Every time she gets coffee at the tiny cafe inside, she can never tell if it's actually any good or if she just loves the view of the cramped and tall bookcases surrounding her. Even if she wanted to bail on this outing with Collin early, she would've had the same answer. "Absolutely."

Before actually settling down in the cafe, Liv takes Collin on a short journey through the narrow three-story bookstore. "Isn't it like that place in Aberdeen?" she remarks as they both duck under the landing to return to the first level.

"Yes, but somehow this is even narrower," he laughs. "I feel like a giant." Once they've ordered their coffee, they nestle by the windows of the cafe, keeping their coats on to guard against the draft. "How'd you land your gig at Dunkin'?"

She regrets telling him the truth earlier at the restaurant. She should've lied and said she got a more glamorous job somewhere. "No one else would hire me," she says. "I applied at this store and everywhere else that I actually would've enjoyed working at but only Dunkin' and McDonald's showed any interest." She hadn't worked during high school at the bequest of Ella to get good grades and she hadn't even needed a job through the first few years of college. Turns out most prospective employers were suspicious of a 21-year-old with no work experience and an incomplete college degree on her resume.

He sets down his piping white ceramic mug. "So you hate it there?"

"Yeah. I can't look at a donut now without wanting to vomit, and people get really aggressive when they haven't had coffee or breakfast," she scoffs. "Other than that, it's fine."

He laughs. "Sorry. I'm definitely one of those people."

"Well, you're different. I mean you live in this state of perpetual jetlag, so of course, you're a grumpy morning person."

His lips twitch into a frown.

"What?"

He shrugs. "Nothing."

"No. What is it?"

"I don't know," Collin says. "It's a little weird you couldn't find something better. I mean, I remember practically throwing a job at you."

She looks down. "Oh. That financial job?"

"Yeah."

Liv's cheeks grow hot. "I wasn't ready for something like that. It was too much of a commitment."

"Commitment? It's a job. It's not like you're getting married."

She shifts in her seat. "Yeah, but it's like a *real* job – a career. If I take on something like that, it feels too permanent. I'm worried I'll get stuck."

He gives a small nod. "Then what kind of career do you want? I can keep an ear out for something serious you actually want to do."

"I don't know what I want right now."

He studies her before taking a drink. "When are you going back to school?"

She blows the steam from her latte. "I don't know. I'm not sure if I will."

"Why not?"

Her answer is different from what she tells Logan when he frequently berates her about this subject. "It just doesn't seem to matter. I don't know if I care enough to actually study or sit in class anymore."

"It'll probably take time for things to matter again, I think," Collin says after a pause. "Have you been writing anything recently?"

"No." The instinct to write comes from the same place within her as the instinct to breathe and drink water. But whenever she sits down in front of a blank page these days and tries to put into words her thoughts and feelings, she finds it too difficult to reflect and drops the pen like a hot iron in her trembling hands. "I'm not sure if I'm even capable of doing that anymore."

Collin frowns before taking a drink.

"What?"

"Nothing. Well, what's stopping you from trying?"

She sighs. "Trying to write? I don't know how to explain it.

89

Actually, I guess that's the problem."

He looks at her.

"I'm not sure if you've noticed this about me, but I'm not the best at communicating how I feel." Ella had called her quiet. Logan says she's cold.

Collin gives a little half-nod. "You're...a bit reserved, I guess."

"Sure, reserved," she agrees. "Well, that's why I've always liked writing. It's easier for me to put things down that way to sort through them. But now, it's like everything's so tangled up inside that I can't even tell where to start. That's why I can't do it. It's not like I haven't tried."

"Why can't it stay tangled?" Collin sets his mug on the table. "I mean, you don't have to fix your thoughts before you put them down. Isn't literature supposed to be kind of messy?"

"I guess..."

Collin leans forward. "Do you remember that Murakami book you got me?"

"Yeah."

He smiles. "Well, most of that story was pretty nonsensical. But that's the point. That's how people are and how they think. And that's why art is so weird."

"Okay sure, but it's not that easy. At least not for me."

He nods. "Yeah, I know. All I'm saying is don't give up yet. When you're ready for it, inspiration's going to strike and you won't be able to stop writing."

She laughs. "Just like that?"

"Yep, just like that."

When they finish their coffee and Collin drops her off at home, she finds herself leaning ever-so-slightly onto her toes as if she's going to kiss him.

"So where does Logan's family live?" Collin asks.

Liv sighs, rocking back onto her heels. Right. Logan. "Hartford."

He puts his hands in his pockets. "Oh. It's a little bit of a drive then."

"Yeah." She could've sworn Collin had leaned in too. Does he want to kiss her? "Thanks for dinner. Have fun in Vermont."

Collin glances at his car in the driveway. "Thanks...um, maybe after Christmas we can get coffee again or something?"

"Yeah."

"Okay, well, Merry Christmas, I guess." Collin grins awkwardly, extending his hand.

"Really? A handshake?" She laughs.

He takes back his hand and shakes his head. "Yeah, I just-"

She hugs him, her chin fitting perfectly in the crook of his shoulder. She'd almost forgotten his scent and he'd been keeping his distance all evening, but now she can smell the pine and coffee. Although the hug lasts for only a minute, she doesn't want to let go. When she takes a step back and his arm uncoils around her, their eyes meet. "Merry Christmas, Collin."

Chapter 13

The car ride is mostly quiet and only filled with music, the alternative rock Logan likes. They have nothing to say to each other, she realizes. As he drives, his movements have tempered to where his hands aren't shaking as they clutch the steering wheel but his eyes are red with dark lines underneath. He must've been out with his friends again last night.

Since they have nothing real to talk about, he barrages Liv with questions occasionally. Questions about her friend the other night. She lies completely in response to each one. No, it was a girl friend of hers. They met abroad. Didn't she tell him before about her trip earlier that year?

With the effort, it takes to answer these questions she could've easily broken up with him three times over. But it's not easy, is it? Like much of her life these days, everything is too laborious, even saying three simple words. *Let's break up.*

Although she hasn't been happy with Logan, she hadn't really considered leaving him until she saw Collin again last night. It's as if she's been living on auto-pilot. She originally accepted the invitation to the Christmas Eve party out of desperation. Even though she's never had the most traditional holidays, her grandfather and Ella were always enough for Liv.

Ella and Grandpa had learned long ago that family wasn't

only about blood. They'd forged circles of kindred spirits that came and went over the years, but the holidays were never lonely. Both of them opened the house to anyone who was displaced during the season. Grandpa had international students from his classes attend Thanksgiving and Christmas dinners and Ella's divorced or stranded coworkers often came when they could. But this collection of misfits wasn't as strong as a real family after all, was it? None of the people who'd benefited from Ella or Grandpa's thoughtfulness or generosity were around when they'd died. No, both of them had died alone.

Liv shakes her head, hoping the movement will dislodge this thought. This entire year since Ella's death, the thought of spending this first Christmas season completely isolated made Liv want to curl up into a ball and hide. Spending the day-of by herself recovering from this outing would be fine. She'll be so drunk tomorrow that it won't matter that she's alone in the quiet house.

Liv's relieved when they make it to Hartford because it means she can breathe if only for a moment before she enters the lion's den.

Logan's family home has always reminded her of a haunted Victorian mansion. The gigantic house has been in their family for generations. This is only her second time seeing it, and she still thinks it looks terrifying even from the outside before the real horrors within become evident.

Logan's out of the car first, parked beside the other Bentleys and Rolls Royces near the seven-car garage. He opens the door for Liv before she completely gathers her coat and bag. He kisses her when she steps out beside him, that familiar salty taste of his tongue making her pucker.

The same things that disturbed her from her last visit are

exaggerated by the Christmas libations flowing freely.

"How are you doing at the firm?" Logan's father asks, holding a glass of Port beside the tree.

Liv dies inside with this question. Logan's answer will ramble on for upwards of half an hour. She leaves his side quietly and goes to the kitchen, grabbing one of the shrimp hors d'oeuvres and refilling her wine.

"How's everything in your world, Liv?" Logan's mother, Janelle, purrs behind her.

Her world. That's truly how Logan and his family see things. They know just by looking at her that Liv's reality is nothing like their own.

Liv quickly takes a sip before answering. "Everything's great."

Janelle's bright red smile widens. "Are you still working at the donut place?" She smoothes down the front of her perfectly starched white dress.

Liv nods. "Yep."

Janelle takes a step closer to her. "Any plans to get a real job soon? Or wait, you haven't finished school yet, right?"

Liv swallows another mouthful and smiles. "That's right." She's noticed how frazzled Janelle gets when she doesn't respond negatively. In Logan's world, the men respond to any slight in anger and the women with a barbed insult.

Logan's brother, standing on the other side of the kitchen, has stopped pouring whiskey to listen.

"We're very proud of Logan," Janelle says. "You probably need to focus on figuring out your own future instead of counting on his."

In other words, she thinks Liv is a gold digger. This isn't new information. Janelle insinuates or explicitly says the same each time they interact. If Liv had any remote intentions of staying with Logan past Christmas she would fight back but what does it really matter at this point?

Janelle eventually walks back to Logan and his father when Liv remains silent.

Liv chugs a bit of wine each time Janelle strokes Logan's fair hair the rest of the day or each time one of Logan's relatives asks her a question about her family. His grandfather has even harsher words for her once she's five drinks in. "I remember when I was his age," he says, narrowing his tired black eyes. "I spent some time with the riffraff before realizing where I wanted to get in life." Again, Liv has no response to this other than to drain her glass as the old man sidles back to the jackals sitting by the hearth.

She suspects Logan is undergoing this exact same phase of his life. She suspects this is why he even brings Liv to his family's house occasionally. Maybe he likes their disapproval. He likes the way they sneer at his cheap, orphaned girlfriend. His family's confirmation that she's trash gives him license to treat her the way he does. Or maybe this is how he's always treated women.

Around dusk, Logan eventually finds her, her mouth stained red, in the family library. She rediscovered it by accident while looking for a place to escape to when his family began singing Christmas carols. It's unreal that such a needlessly cruel and hostile bunch can sing so purely. She's been staring at the pages of an old, annotated volume of *The Art of War* when he emerges beside her perch in the window.

"What are you doing here?" he asks. "Are you ready to go back in a little while?"

She closes the book and sets it next to her. "Yes." She was

ready hours ago.

He glances over his shoulder at the door before approaching her. She turns away from him when he touches her cheek. His hands rest on her knees and he gently parts her legs, standing between them. "You look good sitting here," he breathes, lifting her dress to her waist and nuzzling her neck.

"I want to go home," she says, limp under his hands.

"There's nothing we can do there that we can't do here." He touches the neckline of her dress. "Take this off."

"No."

He yanks her by the wrist and spins her around, bending her over the seat toward the window. Although the movement is violent, he's not angry, just repositioning his plaything as a child would the bendable arms on a Barbie.

She doesn't resist as he lifts her dress up again and tugs down her black tights. She listens to the sound of his zipper and feels the bite of his belt buckle against her skin, clutching at the edge of the window seat as he goes deeper with each thrust, a sharp pain shooting through her body. She watches out the window as the sun dips closer to the horizon. The property is expansive and outstretched before her. She can picture herself running down that field and meeting the sun before it disappears completely.

If only she'd cared enough to say those words earlier, she thinks. Then this wouldn't be happening again.

His grunts grow thicker as each movement becomes more frenzied until he finishes. He pulls her up to face him. "Sorry, I forgot a condom," he slams a hot hand on her back. "There's a bathroom down the hall. Go clean up."

She walks out into the hallway, only then feeling something damp on the small of her back, clinging to her dress. In the bathroom, she wipes away the wetness on her back with the intricate custom hand-towels and discards them in the trash. There are paper towels in a silver tray beside the sink but she doesn't touch them. She tugs her dress off over her head and wipes away the small blemish on the fabric before slipping it back on. When she rejoins his family downstairs, she drains the last wine bottle too quickly.

On the road back to Boston, he asks what she thought of their Christmas Eve party and she lies again, heaping vague, soulless compliments on his neighbors and family. Her body is so loose she almost feels her lips beginning to form those words. "Logan..."

He exits the highway a few stops from reentering Massachusetts.

"Where are you going?" Liv asks, the wine starting to make her head swim.

He drives into an empty church parking lot. He parks before reaching forward and kissing her neck. "I can't stop looking at you," he groans. "You're distracting me."

She stays silent, only opening her mouth for him to invade it with his tongue.

Say it.

But it's so much easier to just crawl onto his lap between the steering wheel under his tight, stinging grip.

Let's break up.

The pressure of him in the same place where there'd been pain the last time, makes her body more eager to melt into his now. It feels so good that she can almost convince herself that he didn't attack her in the library and that she'd wanted him then too.

Maybe he knew better than her what her body craved. But

once it's over and they're back on the road, she knows this isn't true. When he drops her off in front of her house, she convinces him that she's too tired for him to stay over. She showers twice, her earlier hatred budding and growing within her. Although now she's not sure if it's directed at Logan or herself.

Chapter 14

"Merry Christmas! What are you doing?"

Liv sets the bowl of popcorn down on the coffee table, readjusting the phone on her shoulder. "Watching a movie. You?"

"Just out for a drive," Collin says on the other end.

"To Vermont?"

"Actually...that got canceled."

She pulls her legs onto the sofa and folds them beneath her. "Why? What happened?"

"There's a big blizzard that's supposed to hit tomorrow and my parents didn't want to chance it." A car honks through the phone. "So, we're going to have a get-together at my parents' house today instead. Do you want to come?"

She looks at the paused black and white film on her outdated TV. "I don't know. That doesn't seem like a good idea." She's still recovering from being around Logan's family.

"My parents suggested it. They want you to come."

She narrows her eyes. "Why? What did you tell them?"

"Only that I have a friend who's in town and stuck at home for Christmas." There's a long pause and she can hear his turn signal clicking. "So? What do you think?"

She shuts off the TV with the remote and tosses it beside her feet. "Where do your parents live again?"

"Winchester." Another pause. "So?"

She sighs. "Okay."

"What?"

"I said...okay."

"Good, good. I'm glad to hear that because I'm about to turn onto your street."

Headlights flash across the window on the front door. "What? I'm not ready." She leaps from the couch and darts to her bedroom.

"I'll wait out here if you want."

With the phone cradled on her ear, she rifles through the pile of clean clothes on the bottom of her closet floor. "No, you can come in." The door wheezes open down the hallway and she drops her phone next to the pile, replacing her stained sweatshirt with an old plaid dress she doesn't remember buying. She pulls her yoga pants out from under the dress and tosses them before tugging on wool leggings.

Collin raps lightly on her bedroom door.

"Come in," she calls, stepping out of the closet.

"I thought you said you weren't ready," he says, taking in her outfit.

"Yeah, I'm not," she pants. "Let me brush my hair and everything." She walks past him and he follows her, standing against the wall opposite the bathroom while she combs through her hair and washes her face. "This is pretty presumptive of you," she says, peering out at him from the doorway.

He smirks. "You're right."

She turns back to the mirror, quickly applying a coat of mascara to her lashes. "What if I had said no?"

"Then I would've probably stayed with you here to keep you

company."

She ducks back out and stares at him. "You would miss Christmas with your family?"

He nods. It's not a joke, she can see it from his face, but she laughs.

"That's ridiculous." When she rejoins him in the hallway, he beams at her. "I told you I wanted to be alone."

"You're right. I'm sorry."

Liv sighs. "You're really annoying."

"I know." Collin smiles, gesturing toward the living room. "Were you eating popcorn? For breakfast?"

She shrugs and reaches for her coat hanging on the rack behind Collin. "Maybe." She pulls on her peacoat and secures the first two buttons. "Do you want some?"

He laughs. "No, I had a donut on the way here."

She rolls her eyes. "I can't even look at donuts now," she says. Most of the time when she gets home from work, the sickly sweet scent of icing lingers in her hair and skin even after a shower.

"Well, if you have an employee discount or something, I'd be happy to use that for you," he grins. "Otherwise you're wasting it."

"Does this look okay?" She tugs at the hem of her dress. Maybe the green, red, and gray plaid is *too* Christmasey. "Do I look okay, I mean?" She touches a hand to her hair, detecting a small tangle behind her ear.

His gaze softens. "You look great," he says. "Too great. This is going to be really casual. It's only my immediate family."

She eyes his Oxford shirt and cashmere sweater combo, touching a finger to his shoulder, pointing to the burgundy fabric. "I think we match."

He looks between their outfits. "Yeah, I guess we do."

* * *

As they cross into Winchester, Liv can't spot an ugly house. They all look like restored mansions. Collin occasionally glances at her as he pulls into the crowded wraparound drive- way of an enormous colonial. Overpriced ancient colonials aren't a new sight for Liv, but this one seems too extravagant combined with the small, snow-laden forest and frozen lake running behind it. It's too perfect.

"This is where you grew up?" This explains the cashmere. And the nice shoes.

He unbuckles his seatbelt. "Yep."

As they walk together to the front door and Collin leans across her to ring the doorbell, she wonders what the difference is between him and Logan. Maybe it's maturity, although she doubts it. Logan's 26 and Collin 27 - hardly a remarkable age difference. Clearly, they're both insanely wealthy, both highly educated, both good dressers. What if Collin has the same meanness, he only hides it deeper under the surface? What if he just has more self-control to keep it concealed? What if she grows to see this and hate Collin the same way she despises Logan?

A woman with long, straight silver hair swings the door open and outstretches her arms, embracing Collin. "Finally!" The way she hugs him, her head only reaching to his shoulders, is warm, not possessory like how Logan's mom restrains and pets him. She quickly releases him with a peck on his cheek and turns to Liv. "Hi there," she says, grasping Liv's hand and giving it a light squeeze before letting it go. Liv recognizes the gesture. Collin often does this to comfort her. "I'm Helen. You must be Liv?"

"Yes, thank you for having me." Liv steals a glance at Collin. He's rubbing at a small mark on his face from Helen's lipstick.

"Well, come in!" Helen gestures for them both to follow. "I'm so glad you could make the trip with Collin to come see us."

The ceiling is enormous and extends past the staircase to the right. As they step into the foyer, she can picture Collin sliding down that great, ornate banister as a boy.

"Is everyone else here?" Collin asks, taking off his coat.

Liv follows suit and fumbles to unbutton hers.

Helen nods. "Everyone but James and Karen."

Collin takes Liv's coat and hangs it beside his on antique brass hooks by the door. "Great, I'll introduce you to everyone," he says to Liv before they follow Helen down the hallway into the great den.

Liv's entire body grows warm each time Collin introduces her to a new family member and they hug or shake hands with her. Beth, his oldest sister, gives the longest hug and pats her back twice. Beth's husband, Dan, and her twin pre-teen daughters are more reserved but still smile warmly at Liv. When Collin's younger brother, James, and his wife, Karen, enter through the door, they immediately hand him a golden-haired baby boy who squeals with delight in his arms and babbles excitedly.

"I hear you're a runner," Jim, Collin's dad, says when he catches Liv watching the siblings reunite by the tree. He was a hugger too. The way he had embraced her moments ago reminded her of her grandfather.

"I was, yes," she says. "I haven't really done much since

high school track."

"Oh, so you were competitive? That's amazing. I'm training for a marathon right now and it's brutal," he laughs. "Any tips?"

"I'm not much of a distance person," she admits. "I did the 200-meter dash and hurdles."

His eyes widen.

Helen drifts toward them. "Can I get you something to drink, Liv? We have everything."

"Sure, I'll come with you." Liv follows to the kitchen and two by two all the other family members enter the room as well, each pouring a drink, still talking in a hurry to catch up with one another. "Do you have eggnog?"

Helen nods but glances past Liv at the punch bowl at the other end of the counter. "It looks like it's empty. Let me refill that for you-"

"Mom," Beth calls from in front of the oven. "I think you forgot to turn this on."

"I can refill the eggnog," Liv offers.

Helen places a hand gently on her shoulder. "That's so sweet, thank you. There should be a pitcher of mix in the fridge over there." She strides over to Beth and they anxiously prod at the ham.

Liv retrieves the pitcher from the refrigerator, keeping her ears tuned in to James's account of something disgusting the baby, Micah, did. She can only hear fragments between Collin and Jim's laughter.

"I saw Jessica yesterday at the grocery store," Beth murmurs to Helen when Liv turns her back.

She unscrews the top of the carton and pours the eggnog into the decorative punch bowl. She trains her ears on the low voices over the sound of Collin and James laughing and chattering nearby.

"Did she say something to you?" Helen asks in a hushed voice.

Beth makes a soft hissing sound through her teeth. "She asked about Collin. Can you believe that? After what she did!"

At the mention of his name, Liv stops pouring.

Helen sighs. "Don't tell him."

"Of course not!"

Liv glances over her shoulder as Beth makes her way to her brothers with a glass of wine in tow. Helen appears beside her.

"Thank you so much for topping that off," she says sweetly.

Who is Jessica? "No problem," Liv says, biting down on her lip to keep from blurting out the question.

"Do you eat meat?"

"Hmm?"

Helen laughs. "Sorry, I just–I forgot to ask Collin," she says. "We're going to have ham for lunch, but Beth is a vegan so there's a meatless option too."

"Oh," Liv's eyes flit behind Helen to Collin. "No, I'm not vegan. Ham is good for me."

Chapter 15

For such a large house, it's impossible to find a quiet spot. Collin follows Liv into one room only to be followed by a sibling or two and their spouses and maybe a child.

"Hey, how's everything?" he manages to ask Liv in a hurry as Micah toddles into the kitchen, chasing after him. "Why are you still in the kitchen?"

She stops pouring a glass of wine before it overflows. "Yeah, all good," she says with a grimace.

"Did-" He's interrupted by Micah's playful cry as he knocks into the backs of Collin's knees. Collin sets down his drink on the counter and scoops the baby up when James and Karen drift in and Liv vanishes into the living room. Collin transfers Micah to his brother's arms.

"Is everything okay with your friend?" Karen asks, glancing after Liv. "She seemed upset after lunch."

Collin grabs his mug of buttered rum.

"Mom told us that this is a hard time of year for her," James pipes up, fighting to hold onto the squirming baby.

Collin looks at the doorway once more to ensure Liv's not in earshot and nods. "I think so."

"Why don't you go talk to her?" Karen prods. "I think your parents are planning to break out the board games soon."

"Oh god." Collin sets his cup down again and strides into the living room. "Did you see Liv?" he asks his mom.

She turns around to face him, the pudgy arms of another grandchild around her neck. "I think she went to use the bathroom upstairs," she says. She lowers her voice. "Is she okay?"

"I'm not sure. I'm going to check on her." He starts up the staircase, the sounds of giggling children and clinking glasses fading as he turns the corner.

Liv is at the end of the hallway outside the bathroom, staring at framed pictures on the wall. She doesn't look at him even as he walks up beside her.

He laughs when he follows her gaze.

"So you were a band geek?" she asks, pointing to the picture of him in a baggie marching band uniform with a keyboard.

"Damn it," he curses. "I thought I burned every copy."

She smiles.

"Hey, are you okay?"

She finally meets his eyes. "Yeah, I'm fine," she says after a moment. "This is just a hard holiday, and then on top of that, it's the first since...you know...Ella." She swallows and turns back to the picture. "Is that Beth?" She nods to the photo beside his of the even gawkier cheerleader, her braces gleaming in the flash from the camera.

"Yeah."

She scans the hallway. "Which room is yours?"

He points his thumb over his shoulder. "This one."

She pounces on the doorknob.

"I don't think that's a good idea!"

Liv's eyes sparkle with a mischievous gleam as she steps inside. "Oh my god," she says, taking in the posters on one side of the room. "Were you a punk kid?"

The *Blink 182* and *Green Day* posters are damning. "Well..." He goes to the desk and slides a stack of papers into an open drawer.

She sits on the edge of his bed. "You had very interesting taste in high school. It's okay. I was really into *Breaking Benjamin*."

He casts a quick glance around the room. "So what are you trying to say? That you were more hardcore than me as a teenager?"

She grins. "Yeah, I think so."

He sits down beside her. "Are you having fun?"

"Making fun of you? Yes."

He smirks. "No, I mean here. My family's not driving you crazy?"

She rubs her hands into a small knot in her lap. "No, they're great." The edge of her lips twitch.

"You've been kind of distant since lunch," he begins cautiously. "Did someone say something weird?"

She hesitates, her eyes boring a hole into the backs of her hands.

His heart begins to race. "It was James, wasn't it?" he scoffs. "He can be such an idiot sometimes. What did he say?"

She parts her lips and then shuts them again before looking up at him. "Who's Jessica?" she asks after another pause.

A throbbing begins in his chest. "What?"

She surveys his expression. "Beth was talking about 'Jessica' with your mom earlier," she continues. "Who is she?"

He digs his palms into the tops of his knees and takes a deep breath. "She's my, uh, ex-wife."

Chapter 16

"Oh...Since when?" The question spills out even as she tries to wrap her mind around this revelation. She can detect the sweat forming around his collar.

"I–" Collin sighs, still averting his gaze to the floor. "Since May."

She continues to stare at him. "*This* May?"

"Yes."

Her temple throbs. "So, when we were in Amsterdam...and Scotland and you were sleeping with me, you were married?"

His eyes widen as if that hasn't yet occurred to him. As if she was too stupid to put that together. "No," he says, turning to her. "Technically, yes, it wasn't finalized until May, but we were separated for over a year when I met you."

She rises from the bed, feeling lightheaded from the wine and the heat building in her head. "So, I was just some kind of..." She remembers how she opened up to him when they first met. All the pain and grief she'd shared with the man on the plane, while she was merely a rebound fuck to him.

"She cheated on me and left over a year ago," he continues in her silence, moving to stand beside her. "She filed for divorce that same day. Christ, she's already engaged."

"Then why wouldn't you mention all this?"

"I didn't think...I mean, what was the point?" he sputters. "I was just trying to move past all of that."

Or he didn't think it was necessary to go into this with a one-night stand. She turns and bounds out the door.

He intercepts her before she can take off down the staircase. "Can we talk about this? I think I explained it wrong." He glances over her shoulder down at his chattering family.

She pushes past him and takes the steps two at a time.

Helen notices her. "Is everything okay, Liv?"

She's sick of hearing that same question over and over. "Yes, thank you for inviting me, but I'm going to head out." She doesn't wait for a response before grabbing her coat and bag and slamming the front door behind her. She's already out of the driveway when she hears it slam again.

"Liv!" Collin calls, his shoes rapidly hitting the pavement as he approaches. He grabs her shoulder when he reaches her. "Where are you going?" he breathes.

She tries to shrug his hand off. "I'm going back home."

"I'll give you a ride. Come on."

She pulls her phone from her bag. "No, I'm calling a car."

He sighs. "It's Christmas. It'll cost you a fortune. Just let me drive you back home."

The display on her phone blurs through her tears. "Go back to your family. I'm fine here."

She dares to look over her shoulder at the house and sees the front room curtain raised and the outline of figures peering out at them.

"Look," Collin begins. "Everything you said isn't true-"

"Were you married when we slept together?" she shouts.

"Liv-"

"Leave me alone." She turns back to the road, swallowing

110

the lump forming at the base of her throat. The gray Ford sedan shown on her app turns onto the street and approaches.

* * *

On the car ride to downtown, she can't stop thinking about Collin. She thought Collin stood on his own level of kindness and honesty above other men she's known, but he'd been holding something back from the beginning.

By the time the sun begins to set and she reaches Logan's apartment, she's replayed her first night together with Collin a thousand times. Although she believes what he said about his separation from Jessica, part of her can't help but feel used.

"Hey, I tried calling you," Logan says when he opens the door.

She slips into the apartment.

"I thought you said you were going to stay at home today." He clearly must've returned from his parents' house moments ago, his hair still perfectly slicked back and his black coat still buttoned up to his neck. "What's wrong?" he asks, noticing her red nose.

"Nothing. Can I hang out here for a little bit?" She can't imagine going home alone right now. The thought of entering that empty house after dark on Christmas makes her shiver.

"Yeah, okay." He turns and walks toward his bedroom. "I'm going to change. Do you want anything to drink?" he calls over his shoulder.

She keeps her coat on and sinks onto his stiff, black leather couch. Everything at Logan's place is carefully curated to impress but almost unnecessarily uncomfortable. This couch, his bed, almost everything in the kitchen appears luxurious but feels terrible. The TV isn't on, but she stares at the blank screen. "Yes."

He comes out in a crisp t-shirt and black sweatpants. Both must be designer but she can't tell the difference. "Scotch?"

"Sure."

She locks eyes with her reflection in the flatscreen. There's something vacant and haunting about the hollowness of her gaze bouncing back at her. Does she really look that empty?

He sets down two tumblers of scotch with ice on the table and sits beside her, his leg hot against hers. His eyes drift over her as he flicks on the remote. *A White Christmas* is playing on this channel, but it's in color, unlike her DVD at home. It's remarkable how good everything had been with Collin earlier and his family until it wasn't. She'd almost forgotten that being around others wasn't supposed to involve pain.

Logan puts his arm around her. "Aren't you going to take this off?" He begins to unbutton her coat with his free hand.

"No. I'm cold."

He doesn't stop until it's completely open.

She continues to watch the screen as Bing Crosby sings and dances with Rosemary Clooney. Somehow it looks better in black and white. Logan's managed to slide her skirt up around her waist and now he inches down her leggings, sliding a cold hand up her leg.

"Where did you go wearing this?" he grunts into her ear.

She pulls away but he coils his arm around her hips and tugs her onto his lap. "Stop," she says.

His breathing grows heavier and his grip tighter.

"Stop!" She snaps her elbow back into his face, a sickening snap echoing through the room.

He moans, but it's not his usual self-satisfied sound, rather in pain. He relinquishes his grip around her and she leaps to her feet, pulling her leggings back up her thighs. "What the-" he gasps, clutching at his nose, blood staining his fingers. "You bitch!" He bounds toward her and seizes her wrist, twisting it back until it pops.

"Let go," she whimpers, the pain rapidly spreading through her arm. He could snap her hand in this position, she realizes.

His hand flies back to his face. "Jesus Christ! What's wrong with you?" he shouts, pinching the top of his nose.

She rubs her wrist and takes quiet steps backward to the door. "This is over."

His footfalls thunder behind her as she runs out the door.

She doesn't stop running until there are five blocks between her and Logan's apartment. It's late and the streets are mostly quiet, the scene made eerie by the sound of department store Christmas music carrying on the wind. She imagines everyone at home huddled together with their families. She can picture Collin sitting with his beautiful parents and siblings in their mammoth living room, probably on their third pitcher of eggnog.

She leans against a nearby fire hydrant behind her, the iron like ice against her back. Her phone buzzes in her pocket and her heart stirs back into an urgent pace. What if it's Logan?

She pulls it out and almost cries when she sees the caller ID. She presses the phone against her ear.

"I'm so sorry about...can we just talk? Are you okay? Did you get home?" Collin asks in response to her silence.

She wipes at her eyes with the sleeve of her coat, her wrist tender to the touch as it grazes her face.

"Liv? Hello?"

"Yeah?"

"Did you make it home okay?"

She sniffs. "Can you give me a ride?" her voice quavers, breaking completely on the last word.

"Where are you?"

She glances over her shoulder, a drop of shockingly cold rain hitting her face. "I'm on Sudbury, across from Haymarket."

"Okay," he says. "I just got into the city. I'll be right there." He adds after a pause, "What happened?"

Chapter 17

Does it really matter if their marriage was already over in every other sense of the word? Was Collin really obligated to wait to start living his life after the marriage itself was long dead and his wife was off with someone else?

Liv can't decide. But knowing about his marriage somehow cheapens the events in Amsterdam and Scotland for her. Now when she considers their first meeting through this lens, she sees an older, married man preying on a heartbroken girl rather than serendipity.

"Liv?"

She looks at him. He's staring ahead through the rain-battered windshield. That's not what happened, is it? Being with him, she knows he cares about her. "Yeah," she says softly. *She* had pursued him. *She* had wanted him. Hadn't she?

"What are you thinking?"

She shakes her head. "I guess I don't know if I believe you." These aren't the right words. She does believe him, but this doesn't change the way the truth makes her feel.

He glances at her before turning back to the road. "You think I'm lying about this? Why would I do that?"

"I'm not sure. Why did you lie in the first place?"

He opens his mouth and then quickly bites down on his

bottom lip. "I didn't lie to you," he says after a minute. "I like you and I didn't want to complicate things back then. It was too hard to explain."

She thinks back to their first conversation. Maybe she hadn't given him the chance to tell her anything real about himself. Their first interactions were all about her, all about what she was going through.

"I'm sorry," he continues. The patter of the rain is starting to grow fainter. "I know what you must be thinking, but..." he shakes his head. "I swear there's nothing more to it. To me, and to her, it was already over." The headlights flash onto the front door of her house. He parks in the driveway and hangs his hands over the top of the steering wheel.

Maybe the answer is simpler than all that. Maybe the real reason he didn't mention it is because there had been no way of knowing what they could mean to each other. She clasps her hands together and squeezes them hard in her lap until they ache, pressing them into her skirt, still damp from the freezing rain. "Okay."

He turns to her. "Okay?"

She nods. "I–I get why you didn't say anything when we first met." She leans against the door and faces him. His eyes are wide and searching as they carefully survey her expression. "I had no idea you were going through all of that."

He brings his hands down to his knees.

"I wish you would've told me. But maybe you felt like you couldn't. I was a mess that whole trip." She's still a mess.

"It didn't even cross my mind to talk about it. I wanted to be there for you and Jessica was just a bad memory at that point." He raises his hand slightly as if he wants to touch her, but lets it fall back to his lap. "You weren't a distraction or rebound or

116

anything like that."

"Yes, I was," she says in a low voice. "But that's okay as long as that's not what I am to you now." They stare at each other in a charged silence. She can hear her own thoughts flooding and filling the empty air between them. "Were you ever going to tell me about Jessica?" How had the topic never come up on any of those late-night international calls and emails for all those months?

Collin runs a hand through his hair. "At some point, yes. I wanted to tell you. But it seemed...I mean, Liv, what have we been doing all this time?"

The question sends her thoughts reeling. "What do you mean?"

He sighs. "Well, we've talked about what you are to me, but what I am to you? Are we friends? Acquaintances? Because I thought something else was going on all this time." His gaze pierces her. "I would've told you, I swear. But then you were with Logan."

"So?"

"So, do you tell all of your friends your relationship baggage as soon as you meet them?"

"I guess you answered your own question. We're friends, apparently."

He scoffs. "I mean, I would say so because you've been dating someone else this whole time. If not, then where does that leave us?"

She shakes her head. "This is complicated." Maybe they'd both been a little unfair to each other.

Collin drums his fingers against the steering wheel. "So, are we okay?" his voice is smaller, almost too quiet to hear over the fading drizzle against the car.

She sinks further into her seat. "Yeah."

His body visibly releases tension. "What happened earlier? Why were you out there? I thought you were going home."

She's almost completely forgotten about Logan by now. "I broke up with Logan."

He looks surprised. "Why?" he asks when she doesn't say anything further.

She's too ashamed to tell him about who she was with Logan and what she let him do to her. How would Collin react if he knew how long she'd been a passenger in that relationship or that she'd never even bothered to fight back until tonight? Would Logan have dared to treat any other woman that way or did he like Liv *because* he saw how little she cared for her own safety and happiness? "I've been meaning to, but I kept forgetting to do it."

He laughs.

This sound he makes triggers her smile, releasing some of the pressure that's been building between their earlier fight and her confrontation with Logan.

"You have the strangest way of talking sometimes," he says.

Maybe it seems that way to him because she has the strangest way of thinking sometimes too. She pulls down the hem of her dress, pasted against her wet body. "I'm freezing. Do you want to come in?"

He casts a glance through the window at the front door. "Yeah, okay."

She's painfully aware of him huddled on the doorstep behind her as she unlocks the door and quickly switches on the hallway light.

His hair is wet from the sprint from the car to the house.

"Do you want a towel?" Liv tosses her keys onto the kitchen

table after removing her shoes on the creaking hardwood floor.

He follows, leaving his Oxfords behind him and stepping onto the tile of the kitchen. "Yeah, I think I need one. I'm dripping all over your floor," he laughs. His clothes are soaked, but not to the degree of the ones Liv is shivering in.

"I have something you can put on if you want me to throw your clothes in the dryer." She gestures for him to follow her around the corner into her room. She still stays in her old bedroom even though the entire house is hers now. She's left Ella's room untouched. She opens her closet and shuffles through the pile of clean and folded shirts and sweatpants she's accumulated from sleepovers with Logan. He'll probably want them back now at some point. She doubts he'll ever want to talk to her again, though, so maybe they're hers to keep or burn. "Here." She reemerges to find Collin standing over her desk, staring down at her open notebook. She prods his foot with her toe and shakes the clothes at him.

He turns and absently takes the bundle into one hand, using the other to point at the notebook. "You *are* writing something."

She reaches across from him and shuts the journal. "I don't know if I'd call it writing." She avoids his eyes. "I'm going to change. Make yourself at home." In the bathroom, she quickly steps out of her clothes and grabs for the blue towel hanging beside the shower, wrapping it around her body. She can hear the rustling of Collin in the next room as she dabs at her wet hair with the corner of the towel that hangs off her body. Once the goosebumps have flattened along her arms, she shakes out the crumpled red hoodie and shorts from a heap on the floor and tugs them on.

When she opens the door, Collin is still standing in her room.

She catches a glimpse of his bare torso just before he pulls on Logan's t-shirt.

He sees her and makes a face, pointing at the Yale logo prominently displayed on the front of the shirt. "What is this?" he asks in feigned disgust.

She laughs. "Sorry, that was Logan's." She didn't purposely choose that shirt from the pile, but she gets a strange satisfaction from Collin's reaction to wearing another university's colors.

She walks past him and picks up his jeans and button-up shirt from the floor. "Let's get something to drink." She motions for him to follow, tossing his clothes into the dryer and then padding along the floor with wet feet to the kitchen. She pulls a couple of beers from the fridge and kicks it closed with her foot. "He really was an asshole." She rubs her wrist, panging beneath the fabric of her sweatshirt.

Collin sinks into a chair at the table. "Logan? I thought you liked him." He picks up the beers and twists the caps off, a hiss escaping from each one.

She sits down opposite him. "I don't know where you got that idea," she says, taking one of the glass bottles and sipping from it. "I've barely mentioned him to you." It wasn't that she'd intentionally avoided talking about him in her emails to Collin, it was just that he barely crossed her mind when it was occupied by the immediacy of the man sitting in front of her now. It was as if Collin and Logan couldn't coexist in the same space in her thoughts.

He drinks from the bottle. "Yeah, but I thought you two were together for a while - four months?" He watches her for a reaction.

"He was just...convenient." She only realizes how heartless

and cold this sounds after she's said it. She can see from Collin's face that he thinks so too. It's fine if he thinks she's a bit callous. She can't bring herself to tell him what Logan was really like. It's as if she's been paralyzed in a nightmare and only now realizes what he was doing to her. She'd told herself for so long that it didn't matter. Life was fleeting and so was pain, she'd thought.

Collin looks closely at his hands and absently starts to peel at the beer label. "I'm sorry again about today."

She shakes her head. "I'll get over it."

He glances up at her. "So you *are* still upset?"

She is, but not merely about Collin's marriage. She drinks from the bottle. She thinks how pathetic it is that she can't fathom letting go of this young and shallow friendship with Collin. "It's made me think differently about how we met," she confesses. "I'm not upset...sad, maybe."

He frowns at her, thin lines framing the corners of his lips. "Sad? It doesn't change anything about you and me. Not really."

She leans back against the wobbly wooden seat. It's hard to put into precise language why she feels this way, but she decides to try. "It feels like we've been knocked out of balance," she says. "Like I poured out everything inside me when we first met and you were holding back all this time."

He stops picking at the label. "That's not true. I shared a lot with you when we met."

"Only family stuff and then you buried everything about your marriage and divorce." She takes another swig. "I don't know. It–*I* just feel pathetic when I think about it now."

"I don't see it that way, but haven't I made it up to you in the last few months?"

121

She shrugs.

"Okay, well, ask me anything." He outstretches his hands. "What do you want to know?"

Liv studies him, searching for an indication of whether he actually means what he says. "You don't owe me any information. Really, aren't we still strangers?"

His eyes glint with sadness. "Is that really how you feel?" he asks. "I thought we were past this. We're friends, at least."

At least?

"I mean, you've met my family. And celebrated Christmas with us."

At most, what are they?

"And I've seen you cry."

Pen pals?

"We've even been on a trip together."

Her face doesn't break from its stoic expression.

"I think that entitles you to ask whatever you want," he continues in her silence. "I'm not hiding anything."

"Okay...how did you meet her?"

He glances aside as he takes a sip of beer. "Jessica?" he asks, setting the bottle down again.

She nods.

"We were high school sweethearts."

Wow. Who could compare with that kind of history? "She was a cheerleader and you were a football player? That kind of thing?"

He laughs. "No," he says. "She was in the drama club and I was on the swim team...and marching band, as you know."

Liv remembers the first time she saw him stretched out and standing in the airport after they met and thinking to herself that he looked like a swimmer.

"Neither of us were good at either, though." He smiles sadly at his hands.

"Sorry I brought it up."

He shakes his head. "Don't be. It ended a long time ago."

Her body stiffens and she swallows another mouthful of cold beer. "Two years isn't a long time."

"Well," he leans forward, his elbows resting on the table. "She and I were really over long before she left. It just wasn't meant to be. I kind of feel like an idiot for thinking it would last, you know?"

A part of her - a part she hates - wants to pick at that scab and expose it more. She wants to know how he found out about the affair. She wants to know how he felt when Jessica left. She doesn't ask about either.

"What else?" he asks gently, his grin waning.

"Okay." The question just behind her lips is what truly matters and weighs on her. "What was your first impression of me?" She wants more than anything to shake from her mind the way she's reframed their first meeting.

He purses his lips to one side and stares at her. "Do you really want to know?"

Her heart drops. "Yes."

He casts his head down toward the table. "When I saw you crying on the plane, I thought you were having a rough time and I wanted to make you laugh," he says, venturing a sidelong glance at her. "Or smile at least."

This answer warms her. Though it could be the alcohol working through her system. "That's the cheesiest bullshit I've heard in a long time." She fights a laugh building in her throat.

He smiles. "I'm serious. I wanted to know what you'd look

like happy. Is that weird?"

In some ways, it was the response she feared. He'd seen her as a sad, pathetic girl to be rescued. At the same time, it's such a sweet and simple sentiment that she can't truly be upset about it. "Yes, it is."

He straightens in his seat. "What about you? What was your first impression of me?"

She taps on the table with her black-painted fingernail. "I was annoyed with how calm you were," she says. "But I was grateful for the distraction."

"So, you thought I was annoying, huh?" His eyes sparkle.

"Yes, but I was in a pretty bad mood at that time."

He nods. "Whenever I see you, I still feel that way. I just want to make you laugh."

"Well luckily, I don't still think you're annoying anymore."

He laughs. "That's good, I guess."

"I'm sorry if I made things...weird...with your family," she says.

He shrugs. "No, not at all. They were just worried about you."

She assumes he warned his family about her and that this was her first Christmas truly alone in the world. They probably chalked up her dramatic storm-out to that. Her cheeks grow hot as she remembers slamming the door of his family's enormous house. "Will you stay with me?" The bluntness of her question surprises even her.

Collin's eyes search hers. "Tonight?"

"Not like that," she says, scratching her index fingernail along the edge of the wood table. "I just—I don't think I can be alone tonight."

He looks down. "Yeah. Okay."

Chapter 18

He waits in the living room while she brushes her teeth in the bathroom down the hallway. "Do you have an extra pillow and blanket?" he asks when she steps out.

She runs a hand through her hair and cocks her head to the side. "Why?"

"For the couch."

She stares at him. "I'm not going to ask you to stay and then make you sleep on the couch," she says, taking a step back toward her bedroom. "Come on."

His heart races but he obeys and follows her into the room.

She pulls back the covers and slides in without looking at him.

He hovers by the door.

She turns to him. "Are you scared to sleep next to me?"

He is. He's scared he can't get in beside her and successfully fight the impulse to touch her again, to smell her hair.

"Collin?"

"I honestly don't mind taking the couch."

She rolls over onto her side. "You don't trust me?"

"I don't trust myself," he admits.

She holds his gaze. "Well, *I* trust you."

He walks to the bed.

"Can you turn off the light?" She nods overhead to the light on the ceiling fan.

He tugs at the light cord, his pulse quickening, but stands there for a moment in the dark.

"What are you doing?" Liv asks.

He sinks onto the bed beside her, his muscles tensed.

"Are you uncomfortable?"

He looks at her. "I guess I'm a little...confused."

"Why?"

"I thought you were angry with me," he says, "and then you want me to sleep over."

"Let's just go to sleep."

He eases his rigid pose. "Yeah. Of course." He closes his eyes. "Goodnight, Liv."

"Goodnight."

A thousand thoughts race through his mind, memories of the last time they were in bed together replaying under his closed eyelids. He's almost lost to this world he's recreating as he drifts to sleep.

"I don't think I can sleep like this." Liv's voice cuts through his reverie.

"Oh." He shifts to sit up on the bed. "Do you want me to leave?"

"No. I want you here. I'm sorry about everything I said and did today. I've been so confused." She gazes up at him now. "I was scared, I guess."

"Of what?"

She licks her lips before parting them again. "That you – I don't know."

He settles back down on his pillow. "What?"

"I felt like maybe I misinterpreted everything between us."

"You didn't," he says.

She gives a small nod. "Thank you for bringing me to your family's place for Christmas."

He can see her eyes, glossy in the dim light streaming through the window.

"I'm serious," she says. "It meant a lot to me."

He watches her for a moment, trying to discern in the dark if she means it. "I'm glad you actually came. I wasn't sure if you'd want to."

His heart races as Liv leans forward and kisses him. He's forgotten how soft and wet and small her mouth is. He can sense the tension in her jaw as her kiss intensifies. After a long moment, she breaks away, laying her head back against the pillow. "Collin?"

"What?" he pants.

She's silent.

"Liv?"

She shifts suddenly and lifts her head, her eyes opening slowly. "Sorry, I think I started falling asleep." She turns around on her side to face away from him and then slides her body to curve into his, placing his arm around her waist. "Can we sleep like this?"

His lips find the exposed nape of her neck just beside where her hair lays under her like a dark blanket. This desire that's been building since he saw her again threatens to implode within his body. "Yeah, okay," he manages to whisper.

He props himself up on his elbow, watching over her shoulder as her shut eyelids quiver slightly while she sleeps. It was a happy mistake that led to this moment, laying beside her again. If only he hadn't spoken to her on the plane. If only she hadn't had a layover. If only she hadn't left behind Ella's ashes. If only he hadn't followed her to Aberdeen.

If it hadn't been for all that he would've just let her go. He would've probably regretted it from time to time when he reflected on the pretty girl from the plane. Eventually, it would fade from his memory entirely. But because of that happy mistake, he can't imagine losing her. It's strange that he can feel so strongly about a girl who he's barely spent time with in person.

Why *didn't* he tell her about Jessica? After his wife left, he'd been practically catatonic. He'd quietly walled himself off from his coworkers and friends out of this new shame that built up in him after he found out about her affair. He'd frequent his usual bar and drink too much with Adam and Jackson, his best friends from college, vaguely giving answers about Jessica and the divorce when prompted before staggering back to his empty home and vomiting for hours.

Maybe he'd needed Liv on the plane just as much as she'd needed him. Getting up the nerve to talk to her was the first time he actually felt like he was living in the world again in almost a year.

Yes. Maybe they'd needed each other.

Chapter 19

She'd become reclusive after Ella's death although, in truth, it started before that. Liv didn't go out after moving back home to care for her. It had been by no fault of Ella's. Liv had lost all interest in her friends from school while she watched Ella struggle daily to survive.

After Ella passed, Liv's loneliness settled in her like a rock weighing her to the couch and bed. Her friends reached out to her then, but meeting them felt like she was staring at them from the bottom of an open grave, watching as life passed her by.

Having Collin in her house now reminds her how much she's missed having someone else around. His face is painted gold in the light streaming in through her window, his brown tresses glowing red. She's been laying beside him for the better part of a half-hour, just waiting for him to wake up. She's missed this feeling of connection with another person in bed beside her.

Collin stirs, bringing a hand slowly to his closed eyes and wiping it across his face. He stretches toward the sun before opening his eyes. "Hey," he says with a yawn, catching a glimpse of Liv from the corner of his eye.

"Hey."

"What time is it?"

"6:30."

"Why are you up so early?" he asks.

She hasn't been able to sleep more than four hours since Ella's death. Originally, she'd tried taking sleeping pills but she awoke only an hour later, more alert than ever. "Circadian rhythm is off," she says, her tone still flat from sleep.

He looks at her and flashes a coy smile. "Your what?"

She opens her mouth but he holds up a hand.

"I know what it is. It's just funny hearing you talk like that." He rolls onto his side to face her. "You're not sleeping well these days?"

She shrugs. "Yeah. This was the first time in a while that I slept the whole night through. Are you hungry?"

* * *

Over the next week, they fall into a routine. After dinner, she pretends to ask him in only for a drink, but one turns into many and they make it to the bed only to fall together immediately under the sheets, fitting into one another like puzzle pieces.

Sometimes, they'd go to a movie or a museum. She notices each morning with renewed relief that no matter how many times Collin stays over, no matter how many times he consumes her body, no matter how many times he leaves in a hurried shuffle the next morning to go to work, she doesn't feel empty.

Seeing his face in the mornings fills her heart with something she thought she'd lost forever. As she goes about her day, she waits for the emptiness to find her and take hold, but instead, she thinks of Collin. And she thinks about whether he's thinking of her too.

Chapter 20

"Let's do something for New Years," he says. "If you're free."

She looks away. "I actually-I have plans."

His heart sinks. For a second he wonders if he's misread something, or everything.

She sighs. "I'm going to visit my family."

He stares at her, silently.

She nods. "I mean at the cemetery," she says, holding his gaze. "It's this weird thing that Ella and I used to do every year. We wait up with them until midnight and then have a toast. I know, it's so morbid."

He's still processing her words but quickly shakes his head. "No, not at all." He can't decide if that tradition is creepy or merely eccentric. "Wait, you're planning to stay up alone at the cemetery *tonight*?" Any night it would be dangerous, but especially New Years' Eve when everyone was drunker than usual. "That doesn't seem safe."

"I'll be waiting in my car," she says.

Still... "I'll come with you." He still hasn't decided how he feels about this ritual, but he knows he can't let her go alone, for a few reasons. He figures this is why he's noticed a change in her the past week. She must be dreading this New Years' Eve more than usual without Ella.

She gazes up at him. "I know we're, um...seeing each other, but I'd never ask you to come with me to this," she says. "It's really too much."

"If you don't want me to come, I won't. But I want to be there for you."

She leans against the kitchen counter and stares at him. "Really? You want to spend your New Years' Eve in a graveyard?"

"No. I want to spend my New Years' Eve in a graveyard with you."

She rolls her eyes. "I won't be any fun to be around. I'm going to be a mess probably all day."

He shrugs. "That's fine. You're not *that* fun normally," he teases.

She smiles. "It'll be worse than usual."

"Still," he says. "I'm in."

* * *

"I take it you don't believe in ghosts?"

Despite her warning, Liv's mood has remained even-keeled throughout the night. She takes another sip of canned wine staring ahead at the row of slate gray headstones. "No. You?"

Now that he knew that the cemetery was south of Roxbury, he was especially glad that he accompanied her. They'd arrived an hour ago, driving up to the gate just as the groundskeeper was about to lock it and Liv had hopped out. The old man recognized her and seemed disappointed when he saw Collin in the driver's seat. Liv gravely continued talking and the old man's face fell and he nodded, letting them drive in and loosely setting the padlock over the wrought-iron gates without securing it.

"He's letting us in?" Collin had asked as Liv pointed down

the road to one side in a sea of granite headstones.

"He's been here since Ella and I started coming when I was twelve," Liv said. "She had a complete meltdown the first time we did this on New Years' Eve when he tried to kick us out and he's let us do it every year." Her lips had twitched slightly. "I think he felt - feels, I guess - sorry for me. I told him what happened to Ella."

Collin looks at her now as she surveys the dark, frozen pond in the distance. "Generally, I don't believe in ghosts or anything like that," he says. "But if they do exist, this is where they'd be." He'd noticed the worn and cracking headstones and monuments when they wove through the cemetery before finding the newer markers belonging to Liv's family. He's always felt that the streets of Boston seemed thick from the air of a million lives previously lived, but this sense is much heavier surrounded by actual graves.

She leans back against the hood of his car, one foot poised on the front bumper. "I wish I did believe in them."

He follows her gaze to the marble headstone a few yards away.

Milan Zielinski
  January 13, 1970–Dec. 14, 2000

Katharine Adair Zielinski
  May 4, 1969–Dec. 14, 2000

"And hand in hand, on the edge of the sand, They danced by the light of the moon."

The quote inscribed under their names forms a knot in his gut.

"So your last name's from your mother's side?"

Liv nods. "Yeah, Ella had it changed when she adopted me. The Zielinski side is apparently a freakshow and she was worried they'd try to cause trouble if they realized my dad died."

"Why didn't Ella want to be buried here?" he asks softly. Beside Liv's parents' headstone is one with an almost identical design but reads 'Lucas Alexander Adair.' From the dates, he assumes it belongs to her grandfather but doesn't have the heart to ask.

"She thought the whole idea of burial was strange," she begins. "Like, what's the point of stuffing the body in a casket and burying it like that? It turns something so natural into just this toxic-" She snaps from her reverie and glances at him again. "And I guess she liked the symbolism of having her ashes scattered." She gestures to the stones. "Getting buried here was my grandfather's idea. He paid for everything when my parents died and then bought his plot in advance. Isn't that weird? Buying real estate for your dead body?"

He's never really bothered to think about how or where he'll end up when he dies. But now that he does, Liv raises some good points. He can't imagine growing up and only knowing his parents through visits to their final resting place. What does a childhood like that do to someone? Other than her well-articulated thoughts on body decomposition, Liv seems mostly normal. "Yeah, I guess it is a little strange when I think about it."

She shakes her empty can. "Do you want another?"

"Sure, I'll grab it." He takes the trash and walks around to the cooler in the backseat. He returns and hands her a new canned wine and cracks open his second can of Sam Adams.

She unzips her parka halfway. He can see her face growing flushed in the dim lamps illuminating the cemetery. "Did I tell you how my grandfather died?"

He takes a sip of his drink and leans beside her against the car. "No," he says. He nods to Lucas's headstone. "Is that his?"

"Yeah." She gulps down some more wine. "It was a heart attack. I'm the one who found him when I came home from school."

Jesus Christ. Collin freezes. "That's terrible."

She kicks at the edge of the grass with the toe of her boot. "Yeah, it was hard enough losing Ella, but at least we knew she was sick." She sighs. "With Grandpa, we had no idea. It was so unexpected. The idea that your body can just give up on you like that...that's what scares me." Liv's eyes almost flicker and she frowns. "I'm so sorry. I can't believe I dumped all that on you."

"No," he says quickly. "I, um, I can't imagine what that must've been like that for you."

"Yeah, it was shit. It was the worst thing that's happened to me up until the week before I met you."

He involuntarily glances at her parents' headstone.

She laughs, a dark, deeper laugh than usual. "I don't count that since I don't remember it," she says, catching the direction of his gaze. "But that definitely sucked too." She lifts up her phone and looks at the clock on the screen. "This is the weirdest thing you've ever done, isn't it?" She shoves the phone back into her coat pocket.

"No. I've done weirder things," he says, smiling. "But nothing in particular comes to mind right now."

"I shouldn't have let you come. This is a pretty fucked up

thing to bring someone to, isn't it?"

"I wanted to come. I have no regrets." He sips the beer. "This is...nice."

Her laugh is back to its normal, light tone. "You don't scare easily, do you?"

"What do you mean?"

She bit her lower lip. "Well, if you had a friend and he told you that he met this girl and almost immediately after meeting they went to go scatter her aunt's ashes, what would you think?"

He shrugs. "I don't know. Sounds pretty cool to me."

She scoffs. "Okay. And what if he told you the next time he saw her, he celebrated the New Year with her and her dead relatives in a graveyard?"

He grins. "Still sounds like a good time to me." He takes another swig of beer. "I'd be into that."

She lightly taps his shoulder.

As they grow quiet again, he ventures a question. "How did this all start anyway? This tradition?"

She rests one hand behind her, close to his. "I don't know actually," she says. "I just remember Ella bringing me here in the evening on New Years' Eve when I was younger and she talked the groundskeeper into letting us stick around after dark. We ended up deciding to go ahead and stick it out until midnight." She runs a hand through her loose hair, pushing it away from her forehead. "And then we kept coming back like that every year. I have no idea what Ella was thinking or why, but it was kind of nice." She looks at him, her eyes big and wet in the dim light. "We would reflect on what the new year meant for us and then she'd tell me a story or two about my parents."

That's something he can't give to her. "Tell me something

about them," he says.

She shakes her head. "I-uh, I feel like I can't really remember anything about them anymore." She leans against him, resting her head on his shoulder.

He sets his drink down on the ground and wraps his arms around her. "Then tell me something about Ella or your grandfather."

"Okay, let me think. Did I tell you that they co-owned a frame store together?"

"What? No, you didn't. That's awesome! I thought your grandfather was a professor?"

She melts deeper into his embrace, shivering slightly. "Yeah, he was, but he invested half the money for it and he'd help Ella on the weekends. She had worked as a gallery curator for several years, but she'd always wanted to start a business. That shop was her baby."

He hesitates. "What happened to it?"

She sighs. "We had to sell it when she got sick. God, it was terrible. She had that place for over a decade."

He squeezes her and kisses her on the top of her head. "Are you okay?" He pulls back and surveys her red and swollen nose and eyes. He's unsure if she's trying to keep from crying or just cold.

"Yeah." She lifts her head up and closes her eyes, taking in a deep breath of the freezing night air.

"I know this is hard. But you'll get through this."

She opens her eyes again. "No, I won't. I mean, there's nothing to 'get through.' This is how things are going to be from now on. I have to go through everything entirely alone."

He hesitates. "That's not true," he says. "You have people who care about you, including me."

She looks at him sidelong. "How long is that going to last? And how pathetic is that? A few months ago you were a complete stranger and now you're the only person I can lean on right now?"

"Ouch," he teases.

She laughs. "I mean, I'm grateful for you, but what did I do wrong that everyone else abandoned me?" She folds her hands into her lap and stares at them.

"Maybe they didn't. Maybe you only need to ask people for help," he says. "What if I hadn't asked you out tonight? You wouldn't have told me about this, right? You would've come here by yourself?"

She nods. "Yeah."

"You don't have to. I'd gladly go with you anywhere." He gestures to the cemetery before them. "Clearly."

She smiles. "Interesting."

"What?"

"Well, maybe we're both kind of pathetic," she says with a small shrug.

"Oh, for sure," he concedes, chuckling dryly. "I mean, I still have friends but here I am hanging out with you."

"Do you? Have friends? You've never really mentioned any to me other than your coworkers."

"I mean, it's hard to stay in touch with a lot of them since I travel so much, but yes, I still have a lot of high school and college friends who've stayed in Boston." He glances at her. "Do you want to meet them sometime?" Maybe they can be here for her when he can't.

"Yeah, okay. Do you ever think about changing jobs and sticking around here?"

No. He specifically sought this job for the travel. Boston itself had grown too small for him when everything went down with Jessica. He loved hopping on a plane and physically escaping from his problems. It was hard to go around town without coming across one of their old haunts. But he couldn't cut ties completely with this town. He wanted to be close to his family. "Sometimes. Are you getting cold?"

She nods and they move to inside the car.

He turns on the engine but leaves off the headlights. He glances at her as she stares into the darkness ahead through the window.

Without another word, she slips her hand into his and rests her head against his shoulder.

Chapter 21

She's not quite sure who fell asleep first, but she awakes in the early dawn, pale, blue light streaming in through the car windows, mist rising from the pond beyond the headstones.

Collin's eyes are still closed, his hair pressed back against the headrest, his hands open on his lap.

Liv sits up, rubs the side of her neck and then quietly opens the door, stepping out onto the snow. She leans against her parents' headstone and stares blankly at it. Something must be fundamentally wrong with her. For all the stories she heard growing up about Milan and Kat, her parents have never felt real to her. They were a nice fairytale. And there's so much she doesn't know about Ella and her grandfather, but now there's no one to tell her. Ella was her last tether to not only her identity but also reality. She's been floating the past few months, hovering passively above her own life, leaving her dreams locked down below, allowing Logan to have his way with her, hurting her.

It's only in the recent weeks with Collin she feels like she's finally anchored again. She turns and looks at him through the windshield, his eyes still closed. After a moment they open and he blinks, focusing on her. He smiles weakly and then yawns.

She slides back into the car and shuts the door.

"Hey, is everything okay?" he asks.

She doesn't answer but reaches over the armrest between them and kisses him. His mouth softens into hers. When she pulls away, he's smiling at her. "Can we go?" she asks.

"Yeah, of course." He glances at the dashboard before pulling out of their perch at the top of the hill. "Sorry, I don't remember falling asleep. Why didn't you wake me up?"

She watches the headstones fade as they approach the cemetery gate. "I just woke up too," she says. "I'll hop out and lock the gate when you drive out." She jumps out when the car stops and trudges up to the gate in the snow, unlocking and opening it. When she waves him through, she closes and locks it behind them before rejoining him in the warm car.

They're quiet the entire drive. Her because her thoughts are racing too quickly, him because he's clearly still waking up. His eyes are slightly puffy around the edges.

When they pull up to her house, he comes in without her asking, her hand in his from the moment they leave the car. They strip off their coats at the door and sink onto the couch in front of the cold fireplace, the radiator behind blowing heat on the tops of their heads.

Collin closes his eyes and leans back against the sofa cushions, bringing Liv's hand to his lips and then setting it on his leg. "How are you? You're so quiet."

"I'm okay." She's better than okay as long as he's beside her. She lays her head on his shoulder and falls asleep.

Chapter 22

She's not sure what she expected Collin's friends to be like. Whatever Logan's friends were - loud, mean, crude - Collin's are the opposite. The only similarity between the two groups is that they all dress the same, designer handbags and shoes, pastel Polos with popped collars, and merino wool sweaters. Though Jackson and Adam, who have known Collin since college, are jovial, they're not loud and certainly don't raise a commotion about the food or make loud comments about other women in the bar. The girls, Reagan and Dana, Jackson's fiance, speak in their natural voices, not that high, affected voice that Logan's girl friends used.

"So you're from Boston originally?" Reagan asks, turning from Collin to face Liv.

Liv swallows a sip of her Guinness. "Yes," she answers. "Somerville." She's relieved that everyone chimes in to discuss their different neighborhoods and past and future gentrification.

"Collin said you guys met in Amsterdam?" Adam inquires after this topic is exhausted.

Liv is content to just listen while the friends catch up because there's a tightness building in her chest each time she has to formulate an answer. She glances at Collin, his shoulder grazing hers as he hurriedly tries to down his mouthful of lager. "Well, on the plane to Amsterdam," she says. She wonders what else he's told him and she suddenly feels embarrassed. Not only are they all older and more sophisticatedly dressed than, but how had Collin described the crying girl on the plane to his friends?

Collin narrows his eyes across the table at Adam. "Yeah, it was on the flight from New York."

They don't ask any more questions about Amsterdam but move on to pepper Liv with inquisitions about her life, although, Liv notes, any questions about family are carefully omitted. She's not sure if she appreciates or resents Collin for trying to protect her in this way. The bridge of his arched nose crinkles as Jackson teases him into buying the next round of drinks.

His friends begin to trickle out around midnight, each one shaking her hand and both Reagan and Dana proposing a coffee date with Liv sometime in the near future. Adam is the last to leave close to 1 o'clock after his sixth pint.

Once he's gone, Collin leans closer to her. "Okay, so what did you think?"

She smiles. "They're nice."

He raises his eyebrows. "That's code for they're all assholes and you hate me now, right?"

"No," she laughs. "It means they're nice. I have a feeling that you put this together because I said I don't have friends." She looks up at him.

His cheeks are flushed. "Is that bad?"

She shrugs. "No. It's sweet."

He taps his empty glass. "One more before last call?"

She nods.

143

He jumps out from the booth, surprisingly balanced for how many drinks he put down, and his eyes lock on the opposite seat. "Shit. Adam left his wallet." He grabs it and glances out the pub window.

"Go catch him and I'll get the drinks," Liv offers, steadying herself against the table and sliding out beside him. She watches through blurred eyes as he darts out the front door. "Two lagers, please." She leans against the bar and closes out the tab before clutching both of the glasses filled to the brim.

A hand grabs her arm and spins her around, her shoulder popping and the beer spilling from the glass she's clutching. "Logan?" she gasps, pulling away from him.

His face is red, his brown eyes dilated and almost black. "What are you doing here?" he slurs, towering over her.

She sets the mugs back on the bar and rubs at her shoulder. "I'm here with a friend." Even though it's only been a week since they broke up, his face has aged years. Unless he's always looked this rough and she just never noticed it.

His scowl deepens. "Is that the guy you fucked the night we broke up?" he spits.

Her throat dries up. "What?"

"I saw his car at your place until morning."

She swallows. "Are you following me?"

He grips her wrist.

The bartender leans against the counter, fumbling for his cell phone. "Is everything okay?" his eyes dart to Liv.

She nods and relaxes under Logan's grasp.

He tightens his hold, ignoring the bartender. "I came by your place because you were upset when you left. I wanted to make sure you were okay."

"Logan-"

"Did you fuck him?" he yells loud enough that everyone by the pool table a few feet away grows silent and turns to watch.

"Hey, what's going on?" Collin emerges through the entrance, approaching Liv.

Logan releases her and his eyes narrow at Collin. "Fuck off, we're talking."

Collin positions himself in front of her. "If you're just talking, keep your hands to yourself."

Logan strikes his hand out and grabs the collar of Collin's shirt.

Collin's fist comes down quickly and suddenly across Logan's face and they both stagger back in opposite directions from the impact. Then Logan barrels toward Collin, knocking him into the bar.

Liv hears the commotion of people screaming at them and the frantic dialing of cell phones, but she's frozen.

Chapter 23

She presses the washrag against his forehead.

His eyes still won't focus properly. "So, that's the guy from Yale?"

She doesn't laugh. Not even a smile. "Stop. I can't believe you did that," she murmurs.

There's a residual high pumping through his veins even though they left the bar in a hurry almost an hour ago. "I'm sorry. I thought he was trying to hurt you."

She frowns and rests the washcloth in her hands. "He was. But you didn't need to do that."

He can make out a deep red bruise forming around her wrist. "He deserved it," he says.

She puts a hand under his stiff chin and raises it, bringing her face closer to examine the cut above his eye. "Yeah, he did." She pulls back and surveys him through narrowed eyes. "But you didn't. He beat the shit out of you."

He can smell the sour scent of Guinness on her breath as she speaks. "Well, I got in some pretty good hits." He catches sight of himself in the mirror behind her and wonders if that's really true.

She shakes her head. "You're an idiot." One side of her lips is curled. "Are you sure you don't want to go to the hospital?"

He shrugs, taking a harder look in the mirror. "What are they going to do? I don't need stitches."

"I don't know. Maybe they can give you good pain meds or something."

He takes her hand and gently turns it over to look at the bruise. "Did he do this to you before?" The ease with which Logan had laid blows on him made Collin think he was familiar and accustomed to that kind of violence. It isn't until now that he realizes how hard Logan had gripped Liv that he worried.

She notices the burgeoning mark for the first time. "No. I mean, sometimes. When he was drunk." From the way she looks away, he gets the sense this means often. She hands him a bottle of water that's been sitting beside her on the sink counter. "You smell like a distillery."

He twists off the cap and leans his head back against the wall.

"How are you going to explain that at work?" She gestures to his eye and then glances at the cut on his lip.

"I don't know," he says. Thankfully, they'd all gotten out before the cops arrived. That would've been harder to explain at work. "I'll tell them I got mauled by a dog maybe?"

She shakes her head. "Just on your face? I don't think that's how it usually happens."

"Hopefully it'll heal up more over the weekend." He's still holding her hand. He squeezes it. "So that asshole knows where you live?" His stomach turns when he thinks about Logan sleeping in his place beside Liv.

"He's just a hothead. He's not going to do anything now that he got it out of his system."

"I thought you said he was a nice guy. How'd you even get involved with a guy like that?"

She sighs. "I mean, I haven't exactly been in the best

147

headspace lately. He was just upset tonight." She pulls her hand back into her lap. "And he's right. I broke up with him out of nowhere and then ran right to you. I'm sure that doesn't look good."

"Are you kidding me? Why are you making excuses for him? You said he used to hurt you. It doesn't sound to me like that break-up came 'out of nowhere.'"

"I get why he was angry. That's all," she says, staring down at her hands. "I would be too."

"That's bullshit, Liv. If it were reversed, you would never do that to someone." He takes a sip of water, the cold wetness stinging his lip. "Plus, you don't owe him anything. You ended it after dating what? Three months?"

"Four," she corrects.

"Whatever," he says. "I mean I've known you more than six months and I didn't lay hands on you when I found out about Logan."

"You and I weren't exactly dating."

"I know. That's not the point. There's no excuse for him to touch you like that."

"Maybe you should go lay down," she says, standing up. There's a dark stain on one side of her white sweater where her drink spilled down the side before the fight broke out. She extends her hand to Collin.

He reluctantly accepts and pushes against the wall to stand beside her. "Where did I put my keys?" He rubs a small knot forming on the edge of his face as they exit the bathroom.

She stops mid-stride and stares at him. "You can't go home. Not like this."

He walks past her to the living room. "I feel like a jerk. I need to get out of here."

She grabs his shoulder. "First, you're still drunk, and second, you could have a concussion."

"If I might have a concussion, why do you want me to lay down? Get your story straight," he snaps.

She rolls her eyes. "Collin-"

"Where are my keys?"

"I don't know," she groans and sinks onto the sofa. "Maybe you dropped them at the bar."

"Great, so that guy has my keys now?"

"Just sit down for a minute. You're acting crazy."

He exhales sharply and sits down beside her.

"Calm down," she says. "They're probably here somewhere. Can we look in the morning?"

"Yeah," he answers after a pause. "Okay." Once they're in her room, he sits on the edge of the bed in a daze, watching as she undresses, facing away from him in the open closet. When he sees the irritated skin on her wrist, he feels the same rage that compelled his first blow toward Logan welling up inside him again.

She sits beside him in a faded Nirvana t-shirt that almost reaches to her knees. "Do you need more Ibuprofen?" She touches the side of his face with the cut.

"No, I think I'm fine."

She turns off the light and they lay down facing each other on the bed.

He wraps his arm around her waist, studying her face. Her deep blue eyes and button nose.

"What are you thinking?" she asks.

He sighs. "I'm thinking about how much I want to kill him."

"He's not worth it."

"Why did you break up with him?" his question comes out

149

sharper than intended. He's not sure if he wants to know the reason.

She looks away from him. "You know why. You saw how he was tonight," she says. "Even at his nicest, he was still... difficult."

"What did he do to you?" He can see from her furrowed brow and faltering lips that she doesn't want to talk about it, but he can't help pushing.

"It wasn't just one thing, Collin," she murmurs. "It was a bunch of little things."

He often wishes bad things on Jessica when she pops into his mind, but he's never even considered wishing that her new husband, or anyone, would hurt her. The suggestion, the unformed vision that Logan's touched Liv with anything less than kindness burrows into his mind. "You can tell me anything."

She blinks. "There's nothing to tell," she says. "It was a bad relationship and now it's over."

Chapter 24

Being with Collin makes her miss writing. As she gazes up at him, she wants to write about this feeling, the pleasant weight of him. She wants to scribble a few paragraphs describing exactly what shade of brown his hair is. Is it chestnut? Caramel? She wants to write that the color of his hazel eyes is that of embers when you blow on them and they light up with the last glow of a flame.

Those eyes widen suddenly in the darkness and he places both hands on the pillow beside her head. "I think the condom broke."

* * *

Later that afternoon, she opens her eyes when there's a knock at the front door. Something so simple left her feeling drained and exhausted. She throws off the blanket and stands from the couch.

When she opens the door, Collin's staring at her with his eyes wide, holding a white coffee to-go cup in each hand. "Hey," he says.

"Hi. I thought you had work?" She widens the gap in the doorway to let him in.

He steps in beside her. "I did. I left a little early." He extends one of the cups toward her. "It's decaf...just in case."

She accepts it with a bitter laugh. "Just in case? I think it's pretty much a done deal."

He follows her into the living room. "I mean, it's called 'Plan B' because it's not the first line of defense," he says, sinking onto the chair beside her perch on the sofa. "But you're right. It should be fine." He tries to say this all as a joke, but there's fear tinged in each syllable. He glances at the blankets on the couch. "Did you just wake up?"

She drinks the hot coffee, burning the tip of her tongue. "I took a nap when I got off from work."

"Do you want to go for a walk?"

"Yeah, okay."

Outside in the cold, Liv's grateful for the exceptionally hot cup against her palms.

"Look," Collin says after a few moments, when they've turned off from her street toward the nearby park. "I'm sorry about all of that last night."

"It's not your fault," she says. "It happens."

He crinkles his brow. "Really? That's never happened to me before."

"Me neither," she admits. "But it's bound to happen eventually, right? Maybe that's why they're only 98% effective?"

He blushes. He looks like a little boy, especially with his wool scarf knotted around the collar of his coat.

"It was a freak accident and I've taken care of it, so it is what it is." They gravitate toward the bench beside the empty swing set. They sit down beside each other, so close their elbows touch.

Collin settles back against the seat. "So you're not interested in having kids?"

She turns to stare at him. "Like this? Right now?" She shakes her head. "No."

"Yeah, of course. I just meant...ever?"

She slowly inhales through her nostrils. "No."

He shifts in his seat. "Oh. Why not?"

The idea of starting a family only to potentially lose it is too painful to even wrap her head around. "I don't see the point." There's a gnawing dread that formed deep within her when she lost Ella that maybe she's predestined to die young. It feels impossible and beyond her capabilities to build and grow anything. How can she have children and love someone that much all with the knowledge that she's probably going to end up leaving them too soon? "I don't think I'm meant to have a family again." She can see him watching her from the corner of her eye.

"I don't think-" He sighs. "If you want a family, there shouldn't be anything stopping you from having one some-day."

She sets her cup on the empty seat beside her. "I don't know if I'm going to make it to 'someday,' Collin."

"What do you mean?" His expression darkens. "You aren't-are you sick?"

"No. Not yet. But it's only a matter of time."

He frowns. "That's not true. Why would you even say that?"

She gazes at him. "If you were in my shoes would you be eager to have kids?" she asks, her tone growing sharper with each word.

"Don't you think Ella and your grandfather were grateful for any time they got to spend raising you? They thought it was worth it."

These words make her want to jump up and scream at him until he understands. But she's too tired, too weary, from thinking all of this out during the day. "Oh yeah, I'm sure if they could see me now they'd be real proud of devoting their lives to this aimless dropout."

He exhales.

"What?" she snaps.

"Why do you talk like that? None of that's true," he says. "You're just taking some time to put your life back together after everything. There's nothing wrong with that."

She clenches her jaw. "I don't think I'm going to put it together."

"So you're planning to...what? Work at Dunkin' Donuts for the rest of your life?"

She looks down at her hands. "I'm not asking you to stick around to watch," she says. "I don't want you to."

He stares at her, his jaw clenched. "What's that supposed to mean?"

"It means, if you have a problem with how I'm living my life, then maybe we should call this - whatever we're doing here - off."

"Liv-"

"I'm serious. What are you even doing with me? Just killing time?"

He furrows his brow. "I can't believe that's what you think."

"Well, it seems like you're waiting for me to be better and that might never happen," she says, pressing her fists so deep into her jackets she can feel the seams straining. "I'm not going to be responsible for you wasting your time. Clearly, I'm a trainwreck."

Collin stands up, shaking his head when he turns to her.

154

"What have I done to deserve that? I'm only trying to help."

"That's the problem. I don't want your help." With each word she says, his expression grows more downtrodden.

"Okay, I'm sorry. I thought *you* wanted more."

"I don't want more," she says, rising up beside him. "I want to be left alone."

He glances at his feet. "I really hope you don't mean any of this," he says quietly. "I care about you. I only want you to be happy."

And she wants him to be happy but that can't happen if she continues to drag him down. Instead of saying this, she shakes her head. "I think things were simpler when we were just friends."

TWO MONTHS LATER

March 28

   3:40 a.m.

TO: LIVYOURLIFE@GMAIL.COM

FROM: CMITCHELL90@GMAIL.COM

Re: *Now the monkey comes out of the sleeve...*

Liv,

Now that I have your attention with this crazy subject line...

I know you're not responding right now, but I just wanted to see how you're doing? I know next week's going to be hard for you. If you want, give me a call. If not, that's fine and I'll just send you GIFs and weird emoji combinations throughout the week. You know, for moral support.

I'm still in Amsterdam for another two weeks, but when I get in we can meet up for coffee sometime.

Anyway, it'd be good to hear from you. It's boring and cold over here so I'd appreciate any stories of your misadventures in Boston.

By the way, the subject line is a Dutch expression I recently heard from our friend, Finn, and spit out my beer when I heard it. Apparently, it is not a weird euphemism for a sex act, but instead is the Dutch equivalent to "letting the cat out of the bag." Please feel free to use this back home.

In case you missed the point of this rambling email - I'm still here for you...and Dutch is a strange language.

Best,
Collin

Chapter 25

Liv closes her laptop, still smiling. The movement flexes muscles in her face that have gone mostly unused the past couple of months. She picks up her phone and lingers on the open text thread with Collin. He'd already started the barrage of funny GIFs and emojis at exactly 8:00 a.m. on the anniversary of Ella's death. She'd spent most of her day off from school in bed and didn't have the heart to respond. A sense of guilt creeps into the pit of her stomach now seeing the nice messages. She was so cold to him those last few days before he left Boston and now he's gone again out of the country for god-knows how long.

She taps the back of her phone against the cafe table, peering around at the drowsy college boys in their plaid button-up shirts at the table beside hers and then at the two baristas quietly arguing behind the counter. She slips her laptop into her backpack and walks to the tiny table near the entrance, away from the others and dials. With each unanswered ring, her throat grows tighter.

"Hey!" Collin's voice chimes through the speaker after the fourth ring. His enthusiasm warms her to the core even as a draft blows on her from the door.

"Hi," she says. "I just saw your email." She saw it the other day when he first sent it and this was actually her fourth time rereading it.

He laughs and she realizes how much she's missed that sound. "I finally figured out how to get your attention. Good to know!"

She smiles. "Sorry, I just - I felt bad about-"

"It's good to hear from you," he interrupts. "What are you doing right now?"

She surveys the cafe again. "I'm in a coffee shop. I'm about to go to class."

"You re-enrolled?"

"Just in one class for now."

"Which class?"

"It's a creative writing class," she says. "Before you tell me how useless it is, I need this to graduate, eventually."

"I wasn't going to say that! That's great, Liv. How do you like it?"

She relaxes against the back of the stiff, wooden chair. "It's good. But believe it or not, most of the kids in that class are even more messed up than I am. They're writing is something else...not in a bad way." She bites her lip, trying to recall the last short story she critiqued. She's pretty sure the author—the guy who sits behind her every class—is the next J.D. Salinger even though she told herself his story was cliched and unimaginative.

"Yeah, writers can't be trusted," he teases.

"How are *you* doing?"

He sighs. "Like I said in my email, it's cold and boring here, but other than that, it's fine."

She glances at her watch and stands up, sliding one backpack strap over her shoulder and pushing through the front door, starting down the cobblestone walkway.

"Are you doing okay?" he asks after a pause.

Most of the time she manages to keep the thought of Ella's passing from her mind. Usually when she realizes this, though, she feels worse, like she's beginning to forget about her. "Yeah, I'm good." She swallows. "Thanks for the texts."

"No problem. Just sorry I can't be there."

She's replayed the events that occurred when they last saw each other, feeling sick to her stomach each time. They were never really a couple – not officially – but she's sure they broke up that day on the park bench. She'd been uncertain where that left them as friends, even with Collin's regular friendly emails and texts afterward.

Now that she's talking to him, it's as if nothing bad happened between them, like she didn't yell at him like a child to get out of her life. It's not like he'd listened to her. He was quiet for about a week until he checked in with her right before leaving for Amsterdam, even though she'd ignored him.

"Why are you still answering my calls?" she asks. She's stopped walking completely and leans against the redstone building where her class is held.

There's a long pause on Collin's end.

"I said I didn't want to talk to you again." In truth, she can't remember exactly what she said to him that day. The person saying those things, hurting him, was like something dark and evil that had somehow escaped out of her. It was as if she'd watched the whole scene play out in a blur with the audio garbled.

"You said I should get out of your life for my own good," he says each word deliberately. "But I decided that wasn't in my best interest."

She almost laughs at his matter-of-fact tone, but instead tears sting the backs of her eyes.

"Liv?"

She coughs to clear her throat. "Yeah?"

"I'd like us to be friends if that's still okay with you."

A student jogs up the steps into the building beside her. "I think I'd like that too," she says. "I'm sorry for everything I said to you."

"Me too. Hey, Reagan asked if she could call you and I have her your number," he says. "I hope that's okay."

He still doesn't trust she's okay on her own. She casts a glance at the glass door ahead. "Yeah, of course. My class is going to start soon, so I need to get off."

"Okay, I'll talk to you later."

* * *

She can't stop thinking about Collin all throughout class, even as she discusses her critique of J.D. Jr's short story. The notes she took down about the story are bland and hedging, as they usually are. Although she's found most of her classmates' stories disturbing and abrasive, she's jealous of them. Their stories are shocking, but unflinching. Hers are desperate and grasping, and too heavy on some kind of weak attempt at artificial introspection. She starts typing without a plan and what comes out on paper is a meandering answer to a question she didn't know she had. She writes about Ella. And Logan. And Collin. She takes the memories that she's accepted as fact and twists them to play out differently on paper to underwhelming effect. Whenever she reads the words she's typed out, the stories seem so dishonest.

As everyone else packs their bags and begins to leave the classroom, Liv remains planted to her seat. Professor Kinney turns to her desk and, catching Liv's eye, gives her a small smile before folding her stacks of paper into a comically oversized purple handbag.

Liv leaves her things behind and approaches, casting a look at the door and sees no one remaining. "Professor?"

Kinney glances up and grins. "Yes?" She takes off her narrow-framed glasses and drops them into her bag.

Liv's heart beats loudly in her ears. This is ridiculous. "I'm not sure if I'm doing this right," she says finally. God, it sounds so pathetic spoken out loud.

Kinney cocks her head to the side.

"I mean, I'm not sure I'm really getting what I'm supposed to out of this class."

The professor scrunches her nose and peers hard at Liv. "What makes you say that?"

Her face is hot and she wants to rip off her sweater. "My writing seems...bland compared to everyone else's. I don't think my plots are as creative."

Kinney shuffles through the small stack remaining in front of her. "You submitted this for critique, right?" She holds up Liv's paper.

Liv's blush deepens when she thinks about her simple, personal story about the girl searching for her parents. It's such a dull premise, even to her, and the majority of the class had agreed. "Yes."

The professor's eyes glide across the first page before she flips to the next. "I remember I quite enjoyed this." She looks up at Liv. "Why did you write it?"

"It's just what came to mind," she says. "I lost both my

162

parents when I was little and...I don't know. It was on my mind, I guess."

Kinney nods. "I could tell it was personal when I read it. It's a very emotional piece." She sets the paper down. "I don't know if you've been able to tell, but everyone's writing about very different things here. There's no right or wrong way to do it."

Liv shifts her weight and stares at her shoes.

"I will say this, though," Kinney continues. "I like your creative stories, but I think your writing is very well-suited for personal essays. Have you heard of therapeutic writing?"

Liv meets her eyes again. "No."

"It's a way of processing life events and traumas through writing. Some people craft these like personal essays." She shrugs. "Look, I don't know your life story, but to me it seems like you're writing to discover something. There's an honesty to it. If I were you, I'd focus on honing that, instead of trying to fight it."

During Liv's ride on the bus back home that evening, she mulls over Kinney's words. Somehow they're like an accusation, as if she hasn't processed the events over the past few years. She can barely sleep from all the "processing" and replays of accrued regrets in her life.

She throws her bag against the wall once she crosses the threshold and kicks off her boots, meandering into her bedroom. Was the professor hinting that her writing is shallow? Maybe it was lacking depth. Or perhaps it was the opposite. Maybe it was too deep within Liv's own personal experience and beyond the relatability of her classmates and teacher.

Most of time, Liv's not even sure she relates with her own writing. When she reads over it, she often doesn't recognize the cynical and morbid sentiments she's committed to paper. Has her worldview really become so nihilistic? She hovers over her desk, peering at the final paragraph in her open notebook from last night.

She was anonymous. And she resolved to stay that way. That was the surest course to settle into nothingness.

The short story idea came to her after she'd unwittingly stumbled upon her grandfather's humidor while digging through the attic for his old leather-bound books. She and Ella had bought it as a birthday gift the same day Liv walked in and found him, rigid and lifeless on the kitchen floor. She wasn't sure how it even ended up in the attic. After the events of that night, the gift had ceased to exist in her mind until she discovered it last week.

She drums her fingers on the desk beside the pen before slamming the notebook closed. Liv walks out of the bedroom, grabbing her running shoes on the way to the front door.

Chapter 26

She hasn't run in earnest since her trip to Aberdeen. She'd had so much pent up energy and feelings after Collin left for Amsterdam back then and ventured to run only one block around the guesthouse.

She stretches her legs, bending each one before leaning forward onto her knees and peering down the street at the endless worn and sagging houses glimmering from the recent rainfall.

Just one mile.

She takes a deep breath then starts down the sidewalk, kicking her heels behind her as she jogs. Her legs are heavy after all this time away from the sport. She doesn't run for speed now, only to regain the movements, the subtle swing of her arms, the lift in her knees with each bound forward.

The effort of each movement makes her feel stronger with each step. She rounds the end of her block onto the main street leading toward the river.

She remembers running with Ella. It used to be so fun then, sprinting beside her on the high school track on Saturday mornings.

Her throat tightens in the cold air, constricting more with each breath.

She remembers the last time they ran. The cough that halted their workout. The cough that wouldn't stop.

Something catches in her throat as she gains speed down the street. She tries to clear it but it lingers in a heavy knot, choking her. She stops beside an oak tree and leans against it, gasping, lifting her head up, gasping for air.

* * *

"I don't understand. I couldn't breathe."

Dr. Black nods and stares down at the chart again. "Well, I believe what you suffered from was a panic attack."

Liv inhales slowly, releasing the breath back through her nose. "My aunt died from lung cancer. Could I…" She can't finish, her chest rigid from the thought alone.

Dr. Black looks at Liv, her gaze softening. "I'm telling you that right now your lungs are clear," she says. "In fact, the EKG results also came back clear. You're healthy."

She wants to cry. Whether from rage or relief, she's not sure.

"You don't have a history of asthma, correct?"

Liv braces her hands against her knees. "That's right."

Dr. Black sinks into the seat beside Liv on the examining table. "Have you ever been to a therapist?"

Liv shakes her head. "There's nothing wrong with me," she says, although for a long time she's wondered if there is.

"No, there isn't. But the lack of consistent sleep you reported on your last visit and the panic attack suggest you may be suffering from depression and anxiety," the doctor says, typing something into her laptop. "I'll give you a referral. I encourage you to make an appointment."

Therapy seems extreme.

Ella made sure Liv saw a psychiatrist for two full years after her grandfather's death, but she never really understood the appeal. It was always too hard for her to communicate with the honey-voiced woman in those stiff, unwelcoming chairs. She's never been good at saying what she means and the wide, glossy eyes of Dr. Evans only intimidated her. The doctor back then had specialized in adolescent and child psychiatry. Maybe it would be different for her now if she gave it a shot.

Liv drums her pen against the desk, trying to avoid the blank, lined pages of her notebook. After her doctor's appointment, she'd sat in front of her laptop for over an hour, her fingers typing an email to Collin about the panic attack and then deleting everything. She'd done that close to five times before shutting the computer and sinking into her creaky chair. She forgot that committing words to paper was so permanent and she froze once the pen was in her hand.

She had hoped initially that she could finally be honest. Even though he would never see it, she wanted to tell him, just once, how she felt about everything. She wanted to tell him how horrible it had been never knowing her parents and how she did actually want to connect with her extended relatives, but she was scared—terrified—that they wouldn't want her.

She wanted to convey how knowing that family was there and she couldn't have them was worse than never knowing and staying alone. She wanted to describe how he'd hurt her all those months ago and why she'd hurt him right back.

But now, it's so difficult to wrap her mind around any one of those emotions long enough to form a sentence. She inhales sharply, the phantom chest pain from earlier still haunting each breath.

Maybe that's it. She can start with today, with that fear, and work her way back to the day they met.

She scribbles the first two words. *Dear Collin*. There, simple enough. Seeing the steadiness of her handwritten words gives her the courage to continue, haltingly at first and then everything flows. She occasionally pauses to scribble out or retrace a word.

Liv jumps when the phone rings. She catches a glimpse of the time when she answers. Has she been writing for two hours? "Hello?"

"Hey," Collin's tone is cautious on the other end. "Are you busy right now? What are you doing?"

She closes the notebook, leaning back in her seat. "Um... nothing. Homework."

A car honk sounds in the background. "Oh, anything interesting?"

She sets the pen beside her laptop. For a second, her lips almost form the words she wants to say. But she can't. They talk until midnight about Liv's lunch date with Reagan, about Collin's hard week at work and why he woke up too early because his sister forgot about the time difference. She tells him about her unsuccessful run with the panic attack parts omitted. And their call comes to an end like how it used to.

"Are you tired yet?" Collin yawns.

Liv runs a finger over her pillow, pulling the blanket up to her chin. "Yeah, I think I can sleep." There's a pause as she closes her eyes and turns on her side. "Goodnight, Collin."

"Goodnight."

November 18
4:35 p.m.
TO: LIVYOURLIFE@GMAIL.COM
FROM: CMITCHELL90@GMAIL.COM
Re: Graduation?

Hey, didn't you say that YOU ARE GRADUATING next month???

Congrats! I knew you could do it!

I've had to forego most family holidays this year, but I'm putting my foot down on Christmas. I'm planning to get into Boston in a couple of weeks.

Tell me the date of the ceremony and I'm coming no matter what!

Also, are you planning to go to my parents' place for Thanksgiving? My mom asked when I talked with her last weekend and I forgot to call you. She's expecting you, so hopefully you don't have any other plans.

I'll try to catch you on the phone later tonight.

-Collin

November 20
6:22 p.m.
TO: CMITCHELL90@GMAIL.COM
FROM: LIVYOURLIFE@GMAIL.COM
Re: Graduation?

Hey,

Sorry I keep missing your calls. I'm right in the middle of term papers and it's a nightmare.

But yes, I'm finally graduating after years in college limbo! I appreciate the offer, but I'm not even sure if I'll actually walk. I kind of want to just take the diploma and run at this point.

And I know your schedule's really crazy, so don't worry about it.

As for Thanksgiving, I really appreciate the offer and I love your family, but I honestly would feel too awkward without you there to enjoy it. But please thank your mom for the offer.

-Liv

November 21
4:35 p.m.
TO: LIVYOURLIFE@GMAIL.COM
FROM: CMITCHELL90@GMAIL.COM
Re: re: Graduation?

Not so fast!

I'll let Thanksgiving go, but I'm definitely coming to your graduation.

I definitely think you should walk at graduation. You've earned it. But, if you decide not to, we still have to celebrate. I'm going to be there either way.

Wouldn't miss it for the world.

-Collin

December 18
4:35 p.m.
TO: LIVYOURLIFE@GMAIL.COM
FROM: CMITCHELL90@GMAIL.COM
Re: re: Graduation?

I should be in town by Thursday. Maybe we can get drinks then?

See you soon,
   Collin

Chapter 27

"I'm seeing someone."

Of course he is. But why did it hurt so much? "Oh? Who is it? Tell me about her." Liv almost can't believe she's smiling politely. It strains her face so much it feels as though her skin might snap in half.

Collin releases a breath. He must've expected a different reaction, probably the one she truly wants to give. "Her name's Evi," he says. "We met in Amsterdam at that bar, actually." He laughs. "Finn introduced us."

She feels betrayed by this character from Collin's emails. "Wow, that's great. How long have you been seeing each other?"

He looks down at the table, clutching his beer a little tighter. "A few months now." He meets her eyes again after a moment. "I'm sorry. I wanted to tell you sooner when we talked, but it just never really came up. And I wasn't sure if—nevermind."

"What?"

"We didn't really leave things in a good place before I left, and I didn't want this to ruin how well everything's been between us. I figured it'd be better to tell you in person."

She sinks into the booth. "Why would that ruin anything? I'm happy for you."

"I know. But I didn't want you to feel uncomfortable keeping in touch."

Maybe that's how he felt when she first mentioned Logan over a year ago. Warmth rushes to her cheeks. Has Evi been there in the background every single time they've spoken? What does she know about Liv? Did Collin explain how she was his charity case back in Boston? "Why would I feel that way? What did you tell her?"

"No, you *shouldn't* feel that way," he scrambles. "But I didn't want you to get the wrong idea. Other than my family, you're the only person I talk to on the phone. She really wants to meet you."

Her stomach sinks. "She came with you?"

He shakes his head. "No, not for this, but she's flying in next week. We're going to go on a trip with my family after Christmas."

She realizes this is why he's only now telling her this. Of course he waited until after Liv's already committed to spending Christmas day with his family. And apparently Evi. "I'm so happy for you." Bile boils at the base of her throat. "What does she do?"

"She's an anchor on the national news." He appears impressed with this as if it's completely new information to him as well.

She must be gorgeous.

"Anyway, enough about all of that," he says. "Tonight's your last night as a college student, so what do you want to do?"

She laughs. "That's a weird question. It's not like I'm getting married. This isn't a bachelor party."

"Maybe not, but I can take you to a strip club if that's what you really want," he teases.

"No, thanks. I'm good."

"Okay, fine." He settles back into his seat. "But seriously, think of something crazy, and we'll do it. Promise." He lifts his mug to his lips and drinks. "So what's the plan after graduation? Do you have anything lined up?"

She sips from her celebratory cosmopolitan. "Not yet." She glances up at him. "But I'm applying to grad school."

"That's great! Where?"

"You know, all the great ones here," she pauses. "*And* the University of Aberdeen."

He smiles and shakes his head. "I knew you loved Scotland more than you let on."

It's not so much that she wants to go back to Scotland, but rather she needs to get out of here. If only for a year or two.

"So you're applying for English?"

"Yeah, an M.A. in Creative Writing," she says.

"No offense, but is it really worth going to grad school for that?"

She smirks. "It is if I want to get my Ph.D. afterward."

He raises his eyebrows. "Why would you need a Ph.D.?"

She takes another quick sip. "I want to be a professor."

She can almost see him putting the pieces together in his mind. "You'll be a great professor," he says. "That's a lot of school, though."

"Yeah, it is," she agrees with a curt nod.

"Well, you're better than me. I'm glad you're not giving up on what you really want to do." She can read a brief flash of regret on his face. Or maybe it's jealousy.

It was scary for her to decide to commit to this dream. Even just now, she struggled to tell Collin about it as if this is what

174

made it real, not the hours of completing applications or taking the GRE.

Chapter 28

The next morning, Liv's stomach is twisted in knots. She shifts her weight between her feet as she peers out into the parking lot. Fellow students in dark gowns breeze by her into the auditorium.

"Hey! There you are."

She turns around and smiles in relief when she sees Collin approaching. Her eyes barely take in the woman behind him.

He hugs her. "Congrats! Are you excited to walk the stage?"

"Yeah," she says, eyeing the blonde that takes his arm in hers.

He follows her gaze. "Oh, this is Evi. Evi, meet Liv."

Evi's even more gorgeous than Liv imagined. The elvin creature extends her hand to Liv. Rather than shake it, she merely clasps Liv's hand between her palms softly before letting it go. "Nice to meet you," she says with a perfect smile.

Liv fights the impulse to scowl. "Same here. Thank you both for coming."

Collin beams at Evi before they follow Liv into the auditorium.

"I thought she was coming next week," Liv remarks quietly when Evi steps away to take a call.

"She was," Collin scans her eyes. "She surprised me and

flew out early. She showed up at my place this morning." He must catch a glimpse at her irritation because he adds, "Is it okay that I brought her?"

She swallows. "Yeah, of course."

Later, on stage, she's barely able to hear her name get called out for all the thoughts rushing through her mind. When she does walk across the stage, she's overcome with emotion and doesn't look the dean in the eye. She doesn't even look out into the crowd to see if she can spot Collin. The diploma in her hand feels lighter than she expected.

* * *

"Good morning." Adam's smile greets Liv when she opens her eyes.

She's certain he drank more than her, but his eyes are bright somehow. "Hey," she rasps, turning over onto her back, pulling the dark blue duvet to cover her chest. Her head throbs as the first few rays of sunlight penetrate the curtains and she closes her eyes again. "What time is it?" She reluctantly opens them again.

Adam brings his phone over from the nightstand. "9:00, I think."

She remembers watching Collin and Evi leaving the bar for the night. She remembers doing shots with Reagan, Hannah, Adam, Scott, and Collin's other friends before everyone started to peter out. Until it was just Adam. And her. And then they were in a cab. Then on the floor of his kitchen. And then on the bed.

"Do you want to grab breakfast?" he asks, sliding to the edge of the mattress and pulling a t-shirt over his head.

The idea makes her want to vomit. "Yeah, okay." She tries to recount all the details of the previous night as she washes her face and puts on her dress and boots from the day before. She remembers Adam's hot, sticky lips on hers, her leaning into him, panting and on fire.

Shit.

She expected maybe a quick breakfast sandwich and bad coffee to-go, but Adam brings her to a proper brunch in Back Bay. The smell of the gravy and lobster Benedict make her head swim until she takes her first bite and her nausea begins to subside. She looks across the table at Adam, biting into his eggs. "Thanks," she says. "I needed this. I'm so hungover."

He grins. "Yeah, seven shots of tequila in a row will do that."

She eats in silence, trying to formulate an idea of how Collin might react if he walked into the restaurant right now. Would he care? Does she want him to? Of course she does. That's probably why she'd slept with Adam in the first place.

"Congrats, by the way."

"What?"

Adam takes a swig of coffee. "I don't think I had the chance to tell you congrats last night. On graduating."

She nods, turning back to her food.

"So," Adam begins again after a moment. "I don't know what the deal is with you and Collin, but I won't say anything about last night."

She meets his eyes. So Collin *did* tell his friends everything about the first time they met? "Why? What did he tell you?"

He shrugs. "Nothing, but I just - I mean it's pretty obvious there's something going on with you two. Or at least there was, I guess."

She leans back against the seat of her chair. "I'm not - you don't have to hide anything from him. I'm sure he doesn't care." He barely remembered to say to bye to Liv before leaving with his girlfriend. She's become an afterthought to him. "But, thanks," she adds. She doesn't relish the idea of Adam confiding all the details to Collin either.

They leave the restaurant quietly and face each other on the sidewalk.

"Thanks for breakfast," she murmurs, buttoning her coat.

Adam's red hair gleams in the sun. "Of course. Um, for what it's worth, I had a really good time hanging out with you last night."

She actually can't remember what she thought of Adam before they ended up at his place, she'd been so preoccupied watching Collin and Evi. As she surveys him now, she does feel a kind of vague fondness for him, although she's not sure of the origin. She does recall she liked the way he held her last night. And the way he kissed her. "Yeah, same here."

Chapter 29

The other night - or what she remembers of it - replay in flashes through her mind in the shower. Upon reflection, it's easy to follow the string of events leading up to Adam. But now, how can she face Collin? He won't care, she tells herself. She isn't important to him anymore. At least, not in that way. But Adam was one of his best friends. Would that mean something to him?

As she steps out and wraps a towel around herself, her phone buzzes by the sink. She hesitates when she sees it's Collin. "Hello?" she answers.

"Are you ready? We're on our way to pick you up."

She holds the phone away from her ear to muffle Collin's voice pounding through her head. "I don't feel well," she says. "I don't think I can make it after all."

Collin's silent, but she can hear Evi's voice like a tinkling bell in the background. "Are you sick?" he asks finally.

She sits on the edge of the bathroom counter. "Yes."

He sighs. "Come on, everyone is expecting you. And I'm just two blocks from your house."

"But-"

"Please."

She's not entirely sure she can keep from throwing up from

both the hangover and watching him and Evi all day. "Okay," she relents.

"Great! Be there in a few."

After hanging up, she tiptoes to her room with wet feet and grabs at a clean pair of jeans and a red sweater that she's pretty sure still fits. She's towel drying her hair when the doorbell rings.

Collin's alone at the door, but she can see Evi in the passenger's side of his car, beaming at her through the window. "Sick, my ass," he remarks with a smile when he sees her. "You look great."

She finally pries her eyes away from Evi and back to him. "This is weird, Collin," she says. "I really don't want to go."

His smile fades. "What? Why?"

She subtly nods toward the car. "I mean, you tricked me into being your third-wheel. And this is the first time Evi's meeting your family. Isn't that kind of a big deal?"

"I think you're overthinking this."

She glares at him. "I think you're underthinking it. This is going to be extremely awkward."

He leans toward her. "Do you not like her or something?"

She scoffs. "No," she says in a hurry. "It's because I do like her that I feel bad about going. If it were me, I wouldn't be thrilled about meeting my boyfriend's family while the girl he used to sleep with tagged along."

He pauses. Maybe Evi doesn't know that piece of their history. "It's not like that. Enough stalling, let's go. Grab your coat. The quicker we get on the road, the closer we are to eggnogging."

To Liv's surprise, Evi's even more charming with a full audience. Well, if she thinks about it, that's not at all surprising. Her job, after all, is performing on TV. Liv hates the jealousy she feels when any member of Collin's family fawns over Evi. It's only a matter of minutes before Liv is hiding out in the kitchen near the alcohol again just like the previous winter. This time, though, Collin doesn't follow. This time, he's attached to Evi, watching her lips as she speaks in that sweet, lyrical accent.

"Oh, Liv," Helen says, sneaking up behind her in the kitchen. "I heard you graduated last week. Congratulations!" She extends her arms around Liv. "And Collin said you're thinking about grad school?" she asks after pulling away.

Liv sets down her empty glass of wine. "Yes, I'm waiting to hear back from a few more schools."

Helen smiles. "That's fantastic. I'm so proud of you."

Liv wants to melt into the floor. "Thank you," she manages before diverting her eyes to her shoes to keep from tearing up.

"So, what do you think of Evi?" Helen refills Liv's glass.

"She's great, isn't she?" Liv says quickly.

Helen nods. "She seems very nice."

Beth drifts in through the door. "Mom, when do you want to light the fireplace?" she asks.

Helen squeezes Liv's hand. "Let's do that now. Come on."

Unbelievably, Collin and Evi are an even more perfect picture laid out on the rug in front of the fire. Liv's nausea reemerges as she watches him brush strands of Evi's golden hair behind her ear.

Micah appears by Liv's side. "What are you doing?" he asks innocently, staring up at her, no traces remaining of his baby face or pudgy toddler body.

She must've been grimacing at the couple. She forces a smile now at Micah. "Just thinking," she says.

He accepts this response without another word and slides on the floor beside Collin, handing him a picture book and loudly explaining the story.

"Now that you've graduated," Beth begins, sitting on the couch next to Liv. "Are you going to stay in Boston?"

"I don't know," Liv answers. "I'm considering moving. Just for a year or two, for school."

Beth nods. "I think you should. You're from here originally, right? It's important to get out, even if you come right back. I studied abroad in Paris for a year…"

Liv listens to Beth's stories about France half-heartedly, glancing over her shoulder at Collin every few minutes. He hasn't even looked at her since they arrived.

Everyone in the house grows quieter and more subdued after hours of wine and heavy food. It's during this time when Liv is finally alone, looking out through the back window of the kitchen at the scenic frozen thicket beyond the house.

Footsteps approach and Collin stands beside her. "Hey, I lost track of you for a little while," he says, tapping her shoulder. "Are you doing okay?"

She keeps her eyes locked on a small, red Cardinal pecking at the snow. "Yeah." She turns to him. "I slept with Adam." Something possessed her. That's the only explanation she can think of as to why she blurts this out.

He blinks. "What? When?" For now, it's not anger, but confusion on his face.

"Last night," she says. "After the bar."

He falls silent, burying his hands in his pocket and looking away from her and out the window. "Do you like him?"

"I don't even really know him," she confesses. Out of all of Collin's friends, Adam was probably the one she'd spoken to the least.

He sighs. "What the hell, Liv?"

"Why does it matter to you?"

He looks at her again. "You seriously don't get it? Now things are going to be awkward between you two. *And* between me and him."

This isn't the answer she wants. "I'm sorry. It just... happened."

Something dawns on him and his expression darkens. "Was he still there this morning when I picked you up?"

"No! I stayed at his place." She immediately regrets adding this detail.

"Why couldn't you have just hooked up with a random guy? Literally anybody else?" he scowls, shaking his head.

"Is that really what I should've done?" she bites back. "Would you really be happier if I'd gone home with some random guy last night?"

He hesitates. "You know what? You're right," he says. "Whatever you do isn't my problem. Fuck Adam, fuck someone else, it doesn't matter to me." He turns his back to her and walks away, his footsteps dying behind her.

Liv stays in the shadows of the family the rest of the evening. If Collin wasn't paying attention to her earlier, it's as if now she doesn't exist. Evi is tired and settles up in Collin's childhood room, saying she needs to catch up on sleep before they leave for Vermont in the morning. The children have already been laid down for the night.

"Well, I'm going to turn in," Helen says, stooping over Jim and kissing him before ruffling Collin's hair. She turns to Liv. "It's getting late. Why don't you stay the night here and Collin can give you a ride in the morning before we leave? I can set up the spare-"

"I'm driving her back home now," Collin interjects, still

avoiding Liv's eyes.

"Oh, okay," Helen says, making a face at Liv over her son's head before coming over and embracing her. "Liv, it was so good to see you again," she says. "You don't have to wait for Collin to visit to stop by and see us."

"Thank you," Liv responds, daring a quick glance at Collin seething behind her. "Today was amazing." She shakes Jim's hand and waves to Beth on the other side of the room playing a video game with James.

Collin rises from the sofa. "I'll be right back," he calls over his shoulder before walking to the front door and pulling on his coat.

Liv shadows him, trying to stay as quiet as possible. She scrambles into the car and he starts the engine, his gaze steadily focused out the windshield. It isn't until the house is behind them that he speaks. "Are you cold?" he asks, fiddling with the air controls.

"I'm fine." She watches him, noting the crinkling of his forehead. "Are you angry?"

His hands tighten around the steering wheel. "No."

"You look angry."

He sighs. "I'm not. I'm...it's just a lot to digest."

"Collin-"

"You know what? I am angry." He glares at her. "This is some passive-aggressive bullshit, what you did." He's right. He's absolutely right.

"What?"

He shakes his head. "Come on. Adam? You couldn't stand that Evi came early and crashed your graduation. You hate her and you hate that we're together."

Her face grows hot.

185

"You can't stand that she got more attention than you, like a child."

Those words prick her. Even though the age difference between them has been painfully apparent to her at times, he's never thrown it in her face before.

"Sometimes, Liv...I don't know what you're thinking," he scoffs. "What are you going to do now? About Adam? You're going to date him now?"

"He's an adult," she says. "Hell, he's older than me. Why aren't you angry with him?"

His expression flickers momentarily. "I am. But he's not here right now."

"I don't hate Evi," she says after a pause. "But you're right. I hate that you're together."

He pulls the car into her driveway and parks. "Why?" he demands, turning to face her. "You told me you didn't even want me in your life."

"You already know I didn't mean that."

He looks at his hands. "But you made it clear you didn't want to...*be* with me. You can't get upset now that I'm with someone."

"Isn't that what you're doing now? About me and Adam?"

He narrows his eyes. "That's different. I don't care if you're with someone. But you're playing games."

She sighs, massaging her aching temple. "It wasn't like that," she says. "And if that's what you really think of me, I don't know what to tell you." She opens the door and slams it, rushing up the porch steps and digging in her bag for her keys, her vision blurring with tears. She doesn't turn around, but she can hear Collin's car rolling down the driveway.

Chapter 30

Liv tosses her empty can through the open window of her car and slumps to the snow-covered ground. Six cans of wine in two hours. She definitely won't be able to drive home for a while now. The sun has reached past the frozen pond on the other end of the gravestones.

She rereads the inscriptions for what must be the hundredth time since she parked and got out of the car. This time, she can't make it out as clearly. She wraps her coat more tightly around her waist and shivers. She needs to get up and sit in the car and warm up. But it doesn't seem to matter right now. She's not sure if she can stand again.

When she thinks about being here with Collin last year, she truly feels alone. He had saved her from this crushing pressure behind her eyes and in her chest by sitting beside her the entire night.

There's a small metallic rattling in the distance, but she doesn't move, hoping it's just the groundskeeper still tinkering around before heading home. Tears form at the brim of her eye and tumble down her cheeks before the cold air dries them. A rapid crunching of boots on snow sounds behind her and Collin appears around her car. A sob involuntarily erupts through her lips when she sees him and she covers her face in her hands.

His arms encompass her and he lifts her to her feet. "You're going to freeze like this."

She lowers her hands. "What are you doing here?" her voice trembles.

He reaches for her hand. "I didn't want you to be alone."

"Collin..." She buries her face in his shoulder. "I'm sorry."

He runs his hand down her back and hugs her closer. "Just forget about it. I'm sorry too."

She pulls away and wipes her eyes. "No," she says. "You were right about everything and-"

"Liv, let's move on."

She nods.

"You're freezing." He sandwiches her hand between his. "Let's get in the car." He eyes the pile of cans on the floor of the car when he gets in before retaking both her hands into his. "How much did you drink?" he asks.

She leans her head against the seat. "Just a few."

He smiles, but his eyes betray him. "Why did you come here alone like this?"

She sniffles. "I had to. You're the only person crazy enough to come out here like this," she says, turning to him. "What are you doing here? I didn't think you wanted to see me again."

He shakes his head. "We had a fight, Liv. Friends fight, but we're still friends."

There's a sinking feeling in the pit of her stomach when she realizes maybe she's never actually had a real friend before Collin. It had always been hard for her to connect and trust others outside the family, even as a young child. Maybe that distrust prevented her from genuine friendship until she lost Ella. Maybe only after that she'd grown desperate enough to finally let someone in. To let Collin in. "Thank you."

* * *

Back at her house, Collin sets a mug of tea on the kitchen table in front of her.

"Does Evi know you're here?" she asks.

"Yes."

She's skeptical, but he seems tired and she doesn't want to press him. He yawned frequently in the car when he drove her home. "You need to hold onto her." She sips at the peppermint tea, recoiling when it burns her tongue.

"What do you mean?" He yawns again.

"I don't know many women who would be okay with their boyfriend hanging out with another girl past midnight," she says. "On New Years' Eve, nonetheless."

He rubs a hand across his tired eyes. "She's actually in New York right now. She has some friends living there and they invited her to this big party."

"She didn't ask you to come along?"

He looks away. "She did," he says. "But I told her I needed to do this and she understood."

From his expression, she begins to doubt exactly how understanding Evi really is about all this. She'd been very cool with Christmas, but what did she say to him about Liv when she wasn't around? "That sounds fun. Sorry you're missing it."

He smirks. "Oh, I've done New Years' in New York. It's not all it's cracked up to be," he teases. "It's mostly just more throwing up and peeing in the crowded streets."

She laughs. "So basically Boston on a regular Saturday night?"

"Ha!" he barks, his face becoming animated again. "Say

what you will about here, but we are definitely a cleaner city than New York."

She lifts up her mug. "You don't want any tea?"

He leans on his elbows. "No, I'm good." He meets her eyes. "If I hadn't come, how were you planning to get home?"

She shrugs. "I didn't. I probably would've ended up sleeping in my car."

"That's really dangerous."

"I know." She blows at the steam. "I'm really glad you came, but..." She dips the teabag in and out.

"What?"

"But why are you doing all this for me?" She looks up at him. "Why are you there for me? Tonight and graduation and everything else?"

"Liv-"

"I mean, why do you put up with me? I'm a disaster."

He sighs, resting his palm over her closed fist across the table. "First of all, you are not a disaster," he says softly. "But, even if you were, I care about you. I'm not going to let you fall off the deep end without a fight."

There isn't any discussion about whether he's going home or staying over. They slowly drift over to the living room after Liv finishes her tea, him taking the recliner and her curling up on a couch, covered in a throw blanket. She's not sure when they stop talking and fall asleep.

Chapter 31

He loves her like Collin did. This comparison is inadequate even to her, but there have been two types of men in her life to this point. Collin and all the others. Of the two, Adam reminds her the most of Collin. She wonders if this is really only the difference between men and boys. Logan had been slightly younger than Adam and Collin, but his touch was nothing like this. It was selfish and cruel, while the others before Collin and Logan were selfish and cold.

Adam looks at her now, having just pulled away from kissing her lips. "I'm glad you came." He's smiling, but there's a sad supposition behind his words. He didn't expect her to show up. And that was her fault. She doesn't love him, but she does like him. A lot. But in her heart she knows this is short-term. She wasn't numb anymore like she'd been with Logan, but Adam was just another distraction. A pleasant, kind distraction.

Did he honestly think she would miss his birthday party? With Liv's age trailing behind Adam and his friends by six years, she senses that they perceive her as flakey. And that's fair. She's frequently non-committal to their casual get-togethers and late when she does show up. "I told you I would," she says, placing a hand gently on his arm. His body eases under her touch. Of course, she had fantasied about not coming, but only for fear of running into Collin.

They'd had a polite and brief coffee when he first arrived back in Boston last week but he'd been busy since then. She didn't think he was as busy as he claimed, but she too was relieved to avoid the awkward dancing conversation around their significant others. It's what she dreads now as she spots Collin, beer in hand, at the other end of the bar. She's not sure if he caught the kiss between her and Adam.

Adam orders her a drink at the bar before getting called over by a friend from his work that Liv recognizes, but can't place his name. She wraps her fingers around the frosty glass of scotch and ice and hovers at the bar, glancing at the other attendees.

Collin is already talking to Reagan. She wants to join them. She's been careful not to detail everything to Adam about her relationship with Collin. She often wonders if this is worse since he's still uncomfortable whenever she and Collin are in the same room. She assumed Adam wouldn't want to know exactly what Collin was to her, but she wonders if now he speculates on the unspoken.

She climbs onto an empty barstool. She observes as Adam drifts between the partygoers, noticing his body language tighten when he addresses Collin. Collin speaks openly and loosely toward his friend and Liv wonders how many drinks he got in before she arrived. By the time Adam finally makes it back over to her, she's downed three more drinks.

"Why aren't you talking to anyone?" he asks, hugging her waist. He's so affectionate in public. Normally, in any other person she would find this unattractive, but with Adam she enjoys the reassuring pressure of his touch. It keeps her grounded to the moment.

"I got here too late," she says. "I'm sorry."

"What do you mean?" His fingers press gently against her back.

"I missed the cake and everything, didn't I?"

He laughs and sits next to her. "I'm not twelve. There isn't a cake."

That makes sense. It does seem a little silly for a twenty-nine-year-old to celebrate a birthday at a bar with a cake and candles. It also seems incredibly sad not to.

As people approach them, Adam introduces Liv. She listens to the way he describes her to these people and wishes even half of what he says is true. Technically, it is. Every word of it. She *is* applying for her Masters at Harvard, Cambridge, Oxford, Aberdeen, and Boston College. And in the meantime, she does have a fellowship working with the crankiest, most renowned English professor at Tufts. And she did somehow convince this professor to back her research into therapeutic writing.

But why does it sound so good when Adam says it? Probably because he didn't include that sometimes her preoccupation with death was so heavy that even her medication didn't work and she stayed at home for days, missing classes and falling behind on work. Or that before the fellowship, she lost her job at a bookstore for showing up to her shift drunk after one of these dark weekends.

As the night goes on, Liv's attention is pulled again toward Collin. This time when she sees him he's slumped in a corner booth by the bathrooms.

Adam is playing pool with several other friends. She leaves her glass and walks to Collin. He doesn't stir when she nears him.

"Collin?"

He barely looks up at her from heavy eyelids.

"Are you okay?" She sinks into the booth across from him.

He slouches forward, swinging a limp elbow onto the table. "Liv," he slurs. "Liv, Liv, Liv." He has to try too hard to get each word out.

She would laugh if he didn't look so terrible. "Are you drunk?"

He scratches his head. "Yeah...I think I am."

"I'm going to go get you some water." She stands up, but he weakly grabs her arm.

"No, don't go."

She sits again, casting a glance at Adam. Thankfully, his back is to them.

Collin sighs and lets go of her, resting his head against the table. "I'm such an idiot," he says. "A fucking idiot."

She waits for more. When it doesn't come, she taps his shoulder and he jerks his head back up. "What happened?"

He presses his palm against his cheek to stay balanced. "Evi and I broke up."

There's a tension around her chest that suddenly lifts. "I'm sorry."

He shakes his head. "Me too. I'm such a–"

"When did this happen?"

He takes a deep breath. "Right before I came back last week."

She studies him. "Why didn't you tell me when we had coffee?"

He shrugs and leans back against the booth. "I didn't want to tell you."

She laughs. "Obviously. But why?"

His eyes finally focus on her. "I hate that you're with Adam."

"What?" Her voice catches in her throat. "What's that have to do with you and Evi?"

"Nothing," he stammers. "I just hate it. I'm not happy for you two. I hate it." He rubs his eyes. "I hate Adam."

"You don't hate Adam," she says firmly. "He's your best friend."

He stares at her. "Then maybe I hate you." His gaze is so intense she has to look away.

She swallows. "I think you need to go home." She stands up and approaches Adam, placing a hand on his back. He straightens from over the pool table after his turn and faces her. "I'm going to get Collin in a cab," she says in a low voice. "He's barely able to sit up."

A darkness appears in Adam's features and he looks over at Collin. "Okay, I'll help-"

"No, stay here. I've got it."

He chews his lower lip. "Yeah, okay."

Collin's eyes are closed again by the time she reaches him.

"Hey." She shakes his shoulders. "Collin, let's get up. Come on."

He manages to slide to the edge of the booth.

She extends her arm under his and tries to pull him up. "You've gotta help me out, Collin."

He sighs and stands beside her, setting a hand on the table to keep from falling. She's thankful that everyone's attention has turned back to the pool table. Collin clings to her as they stagger through the door of O'Shea's and onto the sidewalk. A crack of billiard balls and a small cheer erupts as the door slams behind them.

At the curb, Liv waves her hand and a taxi approaches.

"Okay," she groans, opening the car door just before Collin collapses onto the seat. "Are you going to be okay?"

He leans his head against the seat.

"Collin?" He doesn't open his eyes. She glances over her shoulder at the bar before sliding in beside him and closing the door. "Can you take us to East Cambridge?" She says, looking at the driver in the rearview mirror. "You can just drop us in front of Charles Park." She lightly pinches Collin's arm and he moves, looking up at her. "Why the hell did you drink so much?"

He doesn't answer but shakes his head and clumsily feels for her hand. His warm fingers intertwine with hers.

When they arrive near his apartment building, his body is heavier somehow and he slouches against her shoulders. "I need you to walk," she says, almost breathless under his weight.

He exhales and tries to balance on his own as they reach the lobby. When the elevator door closes, he leans against one of the walls. She's relieved when they finally make it inside his place and she deposits him on the couch. He relaxes into the cushions with a groan. "Thank you," he says.

She sits on the arm of the couch near his feet. "Do you really hate me?"

He sighs again. "No." He turns on his side and cradles one arm under his head. "I love you, Liv." He closes his eyes. Within seconds he's lightly snoring.

It's hyperbole, maybe. But maybe not, because she loves him too. She watches him sleep for a few moments before she takes his keys from the counter and locks the door behind her as she leaves. She'll bring them by tomorrow morning when he has a horrible hangover and can't remember anything he said to her

196

tonight.

She tries not to react to the relief on Adam's face when she reappears at the bar. He asks about Collin, but she knows what his real question is. She watches Adam play pool and darts with everyone for the next few hours, turning over Collin's words in her mind. She considers the ease with which those words tumbled through his lips when everything else tonight was such a struggle for him.

Chapter 32

The knocking at the door cuts through his head like an ax. Collin opens his eyes right as another tap echoes to him on the sofa. He sits up, propping himself up on his hands. He's still wearing the Polo and jeans he wore out last night.

There's a jangling of keys and the door swings open. Liv steps in with coffees cradled in the crease of her arm and a white paper bag in her hand. She drops a set of keys onto the kitchen table before she notices him staring at her. "Oh, good. You woke up," she says, walking over to him. Her long, dark hair is swept up in a knot at the nape of her neck and she's wearing dark-framed glasses over her red-tinged eyes. "I'm returning your keys from last night, but I also brought food." She sets the bag and one of the coffee cups on the table in front of him.

He swings his legs over the edge of the couch and wipes a hand across his face. "What happened last night? Why do you have my keys?"

She sits down beside him and takes a sip from her cup. "I had to lock the door after I brought you here last night."

He gratefully drinks the coffee. "You brought me home?" He looks at her. "I don't remember anything."

She nods. "You got really drunk." Her lips twitch.

"Oh god, what did I do?"

She smiles. "Not too much." She opens the bag and shakes out two foil-wrapped sandwiches. "You told me that you and Evi broke up."

He rubs his temple.

"Why didn't you tell me before?" she asks. "I thought everything was going well with you two. Also, I thought we were past keeping secrets from each other." She hands him one of the sandwiches. "Bacon and egg," she mutters.

"I don't know." He unwraps the sandwich and swallows a burning sensation forming in his throat. "I was trying to process it. I still am." He takes one bite and sets it down. "Did I say anything to Adam?"

She studies him. "No. What do you think you said to him?"

Since he'd found out Adam and Liv were together—really together, not just sharing a bed—there were so many things he wanted to say (yell, actually) at his friend. None of them appropriate things to air out at a birthday party. "Nothing. Just wondering," he says. "How long were you here last night?"

She shrugs. "Maybe a couple of minutes. You fell asleep right away."

Part of him wishes she'd stayed the night. God, he's pathetic. "Sorry. I didn't realize I drank so much."

She picks at her sandwich, taking a chunk of sausage and croissant with her finger and slipping it between her lips. "You seemed upset," she says after swallowing.

He did say something to her. He can see it in the way she's uncomfortably shifting away from him now. "Okay, just tell me what I said. You're killing me."

She shakes her head. "You just-" she sighs. "You didn't seem very happy about me and Adam."

199

He looks down at his hands. Of course he's not happy about her and Adam. He has a feeling that Adam wouldn't be so happy if Collin took up with one of his ex-girlfriends. Wait. Is Liv even an ex? She's a friend. A very good friend. More than a friend. And he's also slept with her. A lot. "Yeah," he says. "I'm not."

She stares at him.

"I mean, to be fair, you weren't happy about me and Evi."

She considers this and then nods. "You're right. I guess you don't have to be happy about me and Adam."

He drops the sandwich back onto the foil. "Are *you* happy with him?"

She chews, looking ahead at the opposite wall with his TV. "I like him a lot."

"Good." He scratches at the lid of his coffee cup. "Why didn't you like Evi?"

She falls quiet.

"You didn't like her from the beginning and I'm wondering if I missed something," he adds. Evi hadn't been particularly vicious when they called things off, but it was still brutal to discover someone didn't feel the same way. It was especially difficult to not attribute this lack of connection to some imagined betrayal after Jessica. He couldn't entirely be sure of anything Evi had ever told him, but by no fault of hers. And if she had cheated on him, hadn't he made it extremely easy? He was gone for weeks, sometimes months, at a time.

"There was no reason," Liv says, interrupting his thoughts. "She just didn't seem right for you."

"Hmm." He rests his arms on his knees. "Maybe that's how I feel about Adam."

"Collin," she begins in a quiet voice. "Are you really

uncomfortable-"

"No," he says immediately. "Don't listen to me. I'm just being a wise-ass. I'm fine with you two." Or at least he can wait it out. He's estimated they could only possibly have a month or so left based on what he observed last night before he drank too much. She was already starting to pull away from Adam by the looks of it.

She sighs. "Because I don't want this to come between-"

"Stop. I said I'm fine. He and I are fine. And you...you're still okay, I guess."

She laughs. "Okay. Good."

April 25
6:03 p.m.
To: Livyourlife@gmail.com
From: CMitchell90@gmail.com
Re: Answer the damn phone

It's been awhile since I've heard from you. I hope everything's going okay over there on your end. I'm going to be back in Boston in a month and I'd love to see you if you have the chance.

I know you're probably in the middle of dealing with grad school. Have you heard back from any schools yet?

-Collin

April 27
10:09 a.m.
To: CMitchell90@gmail.com
From: Livyourlife@gmail.com
Re: re: Answer the damn phone

Hey, sorry I've missed your last few calls. I guess I was trying to avoid an uncomfortable conversation with you, but I'm sure you've already heard by now that Adam and I broke up.

Nothing happened, we just decided to end it. Please resist the urge to tell me "I told you so."

I hope this doesn't make things weird(er) between you two or between you and I. Oh, and yes, I want to see you when you get into town. I'm especially flexible now that I've started hearing back from schools. So far, I got acceptance letters from Harvard, NYU, Durham University, and Aberdeen!

Anyway, give me a call when you have a chance.

-Liv

June 12

9:55 p.m.

To: CMitchell90@gmail.com

From: Livyourlife@gmail.com

Re: re: Answer the damn phone

Anymore updates since our last call? It sounded like you were leaning towards NYU earlier.

FYI, my flight arrives this Friday around midnight, so maybe we can plan on lunch or dinner on Saturday? Let me know what works for you.

-Collin

Chapter 33

"I don't understand," Liv says, staring at him across the table. "I thought you and Evi broke up."

He shrugs. "We did."

"How long has she been pregnant?"

"She found out kind of late and...I didn't know how to tell you over the phone. She's already six months along."

The room is spinning.

He takes a deep breath. "I'm going to move to the Amsterdam office full-time. To be with the baby."

Her heart clenches. She feels it's going to fall through her chest and hit the floor. "Are you going to marry her?" The words cut her mouth on the way out.

He shakes his head. "No, nothing's changed with that. We're not going to be together. We're just going to co-parent."

She knows that term. It's the word civilized, evolved people use to describe peacefully raising a human being with someone you didn't like enough to continue a real relationship. She licks her lips, desperately trying to quench the desert forming in her throat.

"I'm happy about it," Collin says as if giving her a cue.

She looks at him now and he's smiling. A calm, resolute smile.

"I mean, it was a surprise, but I'm really happy, Liv. I'm going to be a dad."

She tries to match his expression as much as she can, although she imagines how insincere this must appear to him. "I'm glad. Congratulations." All she can see is imaginary chains coiling around Collin's body. He's about to be tied together forever to a new family and ripped away from her. Their time together feels so inadequate.

"So the next time you come to Europe, I'll have my own, real apartment," he says. "Not that work loft."

She nods and downs the remnants of vodka in her glass.

"When are you starting school?"

That's right. She isn't losing Collin. In fact, they'll be closer than usual when she starts school. "September," she answers. "I don't know if I told you or not, but I decided to go to Aberdeen."

* * *

When they arrive at his apartment an hour later, it's in disarray. His escape from Boston has already begun in the form of packed boxes stacked here and there. "Sorry," he calls over his shoulder before darting around the living room and tossing things from the couch to the coffee table.

Liv steps inside behind him, right as he's switched focus to clearing off the kitchen table.

"Drink?" He opens the fridge.

She sits in one of the empty dining chairs, setting her jacket and purse on the floor beside her. "Yes. Do you have any Jenever?"

He pops his head out of the fridge and lets the door close

behind him. "Actually, I brought this for you." He grabs a gift bag from the counter and sets it in front of her.

She pulls the bottle of Dutch gin out. "Let's get this started then," she says excitedly.

He laughs. "No, hold onto that one for later. I have an open bottle that needs finishing, I think." He rummages in the cabinet below the sink and grabbing two shot glasses before joining her at the table.

Sitting across from her now and catching up, he's almost able to forget about Evi, forget about the baby. They briefly talk about the situation with Adam and he allows her to escape the topic.

"Why are we still friends?" she asks after one more shot of the opaque liquor.

He looks at her. "Because I like you."

She rolls her eyes. "But *why* do you like me?"

"What kind of question is that?" he scoffs.

She laughs. "I mean, I'm just curious," she says. "It's not like I'm particularly nice or open and there's nothing special about me, other than I was crying, like, all the time when we first met." She holds his gaze. "But somehow, even two years later you're the most meaningful friendship I have. Why is that?"

He's never stopped to think about it. "I don't know why you have to over-analyze everything like that. All I know is I like you."

She lays her head on his shoulder. "I like you too."

He can smell her hair, that mint and vanilla shampoo she always uses. The same one he used when he had showered at her place. He buries his face on the top of her head and presses his hand against her back, something stirring in him.

That same hungry monster that comes alive whenever she's around.

She's quiet, turning to look up at him, her eyes round and large in the light from the living room.

"Are you happy with us just being friends?" he asks, his words coming out unevenly as he tries to steady his breath.

She leans forward and kisses him, her lips parting for her to make room for him. "I am," she sighs into his neck when she pulls away.

He doesn't know what answer he wanted, but this one disappoints him. She connects her lips to his again, only this time he keeps it going, growing in intensity with each movement between them.

They slip from their seats and onto the floor. Her hands tug at his jeans as he hugs her into his chest. Oh god, he's forgotten how soft and sweet she feels in his arms. He realizes now that he's dreamed this in quiet moments in the night. He's lusted for her since the last time they were together. This time, though, he knows what it is to not have her and he vows to never let her go again.

They twist and curve into one another, their bodies hot and chafing against the rug. This continues until his body finally relents and he collapses beside her. She plays with his hair as he regains his breath, pleasure lingering on his skin wherever she touches.

"Liv," he moans, caressing her mess of hair.

She lays back against the floor, using her shirt as a pillow. His hands wander over her figure as her breath rises and falls. "You do this with all of your friends?" he asks softly.

She smiles. "No." She props herself up on her elbow, placing her fingers on his bare chest.

He wants to frame this image of her on his wall or keep it tucked in his wallet. "Then maybe we're not just friends."

"You're right. Maybe not." She leans down and kisses him, her hair falling over her shoulder and tickling his skin. "I don't know what we are," she says. "And I'm okay with keeping it like that. Are you?"

No. He needs her. He resists the urge to wrap his arms around her and pin her against his body. But he feels if he does she'll disappear like dust between his fingers back into her own mind, her own darkness. "Yeah." He touches her soft curls, sweeping a strand away from her face.

She rests her cheek against his shoulder, casting a glance around the apartment. "When are you leaving?"

His grip instinctively tightens around her. That's right. He has to leave her soon, for one reason or another. "My company wants me completely moved over to Amsterdam in two weeks," he says.

She must catch the sadness in his voice because she peers up at him. "Perfect. So can I crash at your fancy new apartment when I have a layover on my way to Scotland?"

"Of course." He smiles and kisses her.

Chapter 34

THREE MONTHS LATER

Her eyes immediately lock onto him in the small crowd at the gate and her lips break into a smile. She'd missed him like crazy. She quickens her pace to reach him and throws her arms around him. Three months was too long. They'd left things so open-ended before he moved. They didn't talk about their relationship over the phone or in emails, but she constantly thought about it. What he really meant to her and, more frighteningly, why she never wanted to mean that much to him. He grins as his fingers smoothly wrap around the handle of her suitcase. "How was the flight?" he asks, folding her arm into his.

She realizes how she's craved that, the small, comforting gesture. "It was...I made it," she laughs. "That's all that matters."

"You're right," he says. "You look like you could use a drink. You know, to reacclimate to the city." He turns and she follows him down the hallway and out the door of the airport.

"Well, this isn't my last stop, so there's really no point in acclimating."

He narrows his eyes. "I thought you said you'd be here for a week?" He scans the curb for an available taxi.

"Yes. I will. But I'm going to be in Scotland for at least a year, so a week is practically nothing."

She's grateful for the cab and grateful to sink onto the sofa in Collin's apartment when they arrive. It's much more spacious than the previous work unit he was in the last time she'd been here. The décor reflects Collin in everything. Well, almost everything. For every craft wood furniture item or scenic framed photograph there's a baby toy hidden amongst it. "So what are we doing tonight?"

Collin sits into the chair across from her. "I'm thinking food...and drinks. That's about it." He smiles.

She rolls her eyes. "If we're not going to a rave in an abandoned aqueduct then why am I even here?" she teases.

"Sorry to disappoint. I'm not that fun anymore."

"I don't think you were ever fun enough to go to a rave." She sees a lavender-colored sippy cup on the kitchen counter. "How's Mila? And Evi?"

At the mention of his daughter's name, he smiles. It's still so strange to think of him as a father. "They're great," he says. "Mila's perfect."

She tries to picture him with Mila, the fair-haired beautiful baby from his emails. She looks exactly like Collin, except for the soft, pale blonde hair. "How often do you get to see her?"

"We split the week. I'll pick her up again on Monday night and then drop her off early Thursday morning."

She frowns. "You don't get to spend any time with her on the weekends? That seems unfair."

"Well, I go over to Evi's one day every weekend and we play with Mila together. And for the time being, I'm taking paternity leave whenever I have her during the week. The Dutch have a much better paternity scheme than back home."

"Oh." Her head hurts. The logistics seem exhausting. For a moment she wonders if they might as well just be married and living together for all the trouble.

"But, that might change soon," Collin continues, scratching the back of his neck. "Evi's getting married next year. So I'm pretty sure her new husband won't want me hanging around every weekend."

It's quick, but she sees a flash of pain across his face. He never went into detail about how things fell apart between them, but part of her always wondered if Evi rejected his attempts to move forward to the next step of the relationship. Anger gnaws at her insides. Not anger at Evi, but anger at Collin for even wanting that future with Evi. Somehow it feels like a betrayal.

He slaps his hands lightly against his knees. "Are you ready to go eat?"

* * *

She's happy that instead of a rave or clubbing, they spend the night at a quiet restaurant catching up. She hasn't realized how much time had passed until she was sitting across from him and spewing out all the latest news from Boston. Jackson and Dana are expecting their first kid, didn't they tell him? Adam's dating some girl in law school. No, Liv's not upset about it. She and Adam were never serious. Collin shifts uncomfortably at the talk about Adam and Liv switches to Collin's life.

He tells her how life's looking for him now. Most of the time, he doesn't know what he's doing with Mila, constantly calling his mom and Evi for help when he has her. It's lonely for him to be in Amsterdam full-time now. Before he moved here, he wasn't too bothered by the quiet nights and weekends because he knew he'd be going home in a month or two.

"If it makes you feel any better," Liv says to this. "You're still my only real friend back home, even though you don't live there anymore."

He laughs, finishing his wine. "That doesn't make me feel better. That makes me sad. What about Reagan?"

"She got a little distant after everything ended with Adam." There weren't any bad feelings, but of course, it created some discernible tension in their group. Liv eventually quietly resolved never to intrude upon them again. Now that she's across the Atlantic that won't be so difficult.

They take their time walking along the street by the canal. They've finally almost caught up on everything that's happened since they were last together by the time they return to Collin's apartment.

He hands her a glass of water and sits down on the sofa across from her. "How do you feel about going for a drive tomorrow?" he asks. "The moorlands are gorgeous this time of year and there's a castle out there too."

She doesn't know what the moorlands are, but she nods. "Sounds great."

He glances at the clock on the opposite wall. "You must be exhausted. I made up the bed for you."

She notices the stack of folded blankets and pillows beside him on the couch for the first time. She shouldn't be surprised. Collin doesn't want to be presumptuous. After all, she was the one who'd pushed him away. "Yeah, I'm beat." She stands up and he mirrors the movement, extending toward her for an awkward hug.

"Goodnight, Liv."

She pulls away, avoiding his eyes. "Goodnight."

Chapter 35

Feeling Collin's presence in the living room next door had made for a sleepless night. A cold walk through the rolling and unending fields of heather the next morning brightened her eyes, but then she was weighed down with sleepiness from two helpings of Dutch apple pie after lunch.

"You're quiet," Collin finally says when they arrive back into the city. He carried the weight of conversation through most of the day.

She rubs at her eyes. "I think I just need to lay down for a bit before dinner if that's okay."

"Yeah, of course."

Back in his room, Liv lays alone in the bed, listening as he taps on his computer on the other side of the wall. This frustration has been building in her since she saw him the night before and she feels it ripping away at her insides with each passing moment. She emerges after an hour, still without having shut her eyes.

Collin's sitting on the sofa, propping his laptop on his lap. He smiles when he sees her. "Hey. Are you feeling better?"

She yawns. "Yeah." She sits beside him. "Anything fun?" She gestures to his screen.

He closes the laptop and sets it on the coffee table. "Not

really. I owe my parents an email...or two," he says. "Are you hungry?"

She reaches over and takes his hand into hers. She traces the lines in his palm, hoping they indicate a long and full life.

He brings his other hand to her cheek and tucks her hair behind her ear.

Her mouth finds his. For several moments, with his lips pressed against hers, she loses track of when and where she is.

It's only when he pulls away that she realizes they've somehow made it to his bed.

"What's wrong?" she asks breathlessly, leaning against a tangle of pillows.

He looks into her eyes. "I don't want to do this again if we're not more to each other."

She searches his expression. "What does 'more' mean to you?"

His hand runs through her hair. "I want to be with you, Liv." His fingers gently trace the side of her neck. "Not just for tonight."

She shifts onto her side. "I don't want you to depend on me," she says quietly.

His lips graze her neck. "It's too late for that. I already depend on you."

She pushes against his chest. "Stop."

He leans back. "I'm sorry." His voice is low and gentle against her ear. "Why?"

She turns her head away from him. "I don't want you to expect me to be around."

There's a long pause and his arms wrap around her. "Why would you say that?" he says finally, his voice nearly breaks on this question. "Is something...wrong?"

She looks back at him. "No."

He furrows his brow. "Then why? Why shouldn't I count on you being around?"

The explanation, the constant chorus in her mind for the past years, will sound ridiculous if spoken. But she can't resist. "Every single person in my family is gone," she says. "I just have this feeling—" she swallows. "I just *know* that something bad's going to happen to me too." The words scare her even more when said aloud and she shudders.

He runs a finger along her cheek. "You're going to be okay," he says. "You're going to be better than okay. You're going to live a freakishly long and deliriously happy life." He smiles.

Her throat tightens and she buries her face in Collin's chest. She knows his words mean nothing. There's no real reassurance in them. She could die this very moment, tucked in his arms. She could get hit by a bus tomorrow. Or find out she has lung cancer like Ella. His words, even his thoughts, cannot protect her. Or worse, *he* could die. In the canal. In his home. In a car or a plane crash. And then what? A lump forms in her throat. A tightness seizes her chest. Then, she'd be alone again. Truly alone. Irreparably alone. For her, that's when time would stop.

He quietly holds her, his hands trailing through her tresses down her back. "Stay with me," he says.

Collin holding her like this, so closely as if he's scared she'll disappear before his eyes, does bring her some true comfort, though. Since Ella's death, she's feared one thing more than death itself. She's feared the idea that she could leave this earth now, with all her loved ones gone, and no one would truly care.

Collin kisses the top of her head.

Collin would care.

Chapter 36

SIX MONTHS LATER

"Have you been able to find sufficient sources for your topic?"

Liv bounces her leg under the table across from Professor Harding. "Yes," she says. "There's a lot of research relevant to my argument." She glances at her watch. Collin landed over an hour ago.

Harding nods and surveys his computer screen. "Okay, well, do you have any questions at this point?" he asks. "It seems like you're headed down the right path."

"No, I think I'm good for now, Professor." She stands and extends her hand.

Harding shakes it with a smile. "Let me know when you want to meet next week to go over your annotated bibliography and abstract and we'll set it up."

Once she's out of his office, she practically sprints from the gray, towering building and across the lawn, pulling the strap of her bag further up her shoulder.

She spots Collin sitting on the concrete ledge in front of a small chapel. He jumps to his feet when he sees her. She throws her arms around him. "Sorry I'm so late!" she exclaims, her voice muffled against his neck.

His arms squeeze her waist. "No, it's fine." They pull away at the same time, his smile bigger than ever. "I was just admiring the unusually large seagulls."

She laughs. "Yes, one of the many quirks of Aberdeen. I'm pretty sure it was one of those over there that snatched my sandwich last week."

He turns and eyes one of the birds meandering toward the chapel entrance. "How'd the meeting with your advisor go?" He takes her hand and tucks it into his.

"Good. But this is only the beginning. Finishing the actual thesis is going to take a while." She leans forward and kisses him. Being apart for months at a time was natural to them by now. But since she'd moved only four hours away from him, she resented any time not spent together. Not much has truly changed, only that they were now together for real this time. There was no question if they would kiss when reunited or walk hand in hand around town. There was no question that they would sleep in the same bed and have sex each time they visited one another.

"Did you drop your stuff off at my apartment?" she asks, leading him down the cobblestone road past the university bookstore.

He nods. "Yeah. Your roommate wasn't there."

"She's out of town this weekend." She tightens her grasp around his fingers. "Let's go grab something to eat."

He tugs her in the direction of her apartment. "Before that, I have something to show you. I left it at your apartment."

"Oh?" She lets him guide her down the street, asking about the flight and about Mila.

When they reach her place, Collin rushes through the door

first. "Let me go grab it," he says, darting for her room. He emerges seconds later with a huge grin, rolling out a pastel blue bicycle.

"What?" She runs over, laughing. "How?"

He shrugs. "I know you've been literally running around like crazy between school and your workshops across town. And my flight got in early, so I stopped by that bike shop near the beach." He dings the bell. "Do you like it?"

She kisses his cheek. "This is perfect! Thank you."

"What?" he asks when he notices Liv staring at the pedals.

"Well, I just – I haven't ridden a bike since the first day we met." She grips the handlebars. This will make her life so much easier, though. She can't even remember how many buses she's missed because she was walking too slow.

Collin pats the seat. "You never forget once you learn. Try it out and let's see if it's a good fit."

She climbs onto the seat, balancing with her hand on Collin's shoulder.

"Too high?" he asks, taking a step back and surveying her.

With one foot still on the ground, she pedals with the other. "No, I think it's perfect."

His smile grows. "Great, let's go out for a test ride."

He brings her to the park across the street, rolling the bicycle along the brick street beside him. The sun sets early these days and not many people frequent the park this close to dark. A couple of students quickly bound across the lawn, bundled in their thick coats buttoned to the neck.

"Okay, you know the drill," Collin says once they've reached a tree. He holds the bike in place.

She laughs and mounts the seat. "I'm scared, but if I don't crash, this bike will save me a ton of time."

He grips the handle with both hands, his knuckles red from the cold. "You're not going to crash. Remember, you've already done this and nothing bad happened."

True. She'd felt so light that day when she managed to cycle past Collin on the pathway. There had been a couple of close calls, but she always corrected before a tumble.

"Shit, I actually got you a helmet too, but I left it on your bed."

"Ah-ha!" Liv taps his hand still wrapped around the bike. "So you *do* think I'll crash."

He shakes his head, smirking. "No, but eventually you'll probably accidentally steer into a tree or something. Okay, let's do this." He pulls the bike, walking backward and glancing over his shoulder before releasing it.

Liv pedals hard, trying to outpace Collin as he jogs beside her.

"I give up!" he pants, bending over on his knees and laughing.

She makes a big loop around him. "You're right. I'm clearly amazing at this." She brakes in front of him and steps down.

He wraps her in a hug. "Yes, you are. And you look cold. Let's go."

"Yeah, let's take this back and then grab something to eat."

* * *

But they don't get something to eat. Instead, they wind their way to her apartment and tear away at each other as soon as they cross the threshold. They barely make it to the bed before falling together, their bodies tangling in the sheets.

"I missed you." She curls her body into his.

His chest rises and falls rapidly, still trying to regain his breath. "I missed you too." He smiles at her as she looks up at him.

She lays her head back against his shoulder. "I was thinking about that earlier," she says. "The whole time we've known each other we've been apart for months at a time. But now it feels like forever even if it's only a week or two." She glances at him. "Why is that?"

He trails his fingers along her arm before hugging her closer. "It's different between us this time."

"Is it?"

"I think so." He stares thoughtfully at the wall on the other side of the room. Other than the university poster tacked up by her desk, she hasn't bothered to really decorate the place even though it's already been six months. It's like she doesn't want to leave any trace wherever she goes. After months of overnight stays at his place in Amsterdam, he can't think of one item of hers that remains. She doesn't leave so much as a lipstick or shampoo bottle behind.

"What time is it?" She reaches for her phone on the nightstand. "I have my workshop at eight o'clock."

His eyes drift to where the wool blanket meets her collarbone. "Can I come with you?"

Liv sits up, tugging her sweater over her head. "Of course, if you don't mind sitting there," she says. "We're not going to have time to eat before. Let's grab something on the way back if that's okay."

Despite their growling stomachs, Liv's in good spirits on the cab ride to the workshop. She lays her head on his shoulder in the backseat, plugging her fingers into his. When the car stops in front of a squat graystone church, she guides him inside and

221

to a large recreational room. He helps her set up the folding chairs and place snacks, pens, and unused notebooks on a long table by the entrance.

He sits on a seat in the very back of the room while people, young and old, trickle in, unwinding their scarves and hugging Liv. One girl, maybe high school age, bursts into the church, wiping her eyes and dramatically throwing her arms around Liv. As they talk, Liv's expression darkens. She nods and the girl leaves as a small group of elderly men appear and shake her hand.

Once most of the seats are full, Liv pauses with her back turned to the room, gripping the edge of the table. Collin stands, ready to go to her, but in a moment she turns around and addresses the room, her smile dimmer than before.

He sinks back into the plastic chair as she introduces those who are new to the group and discusses the benefits of narrative nonfiction as a means to heal from personal trauma.

A sense of warmth and pride swell in him as he listens to her recount her experience with the crowd. He knows it isn't easy for her to talk about this part of her life. But the people who hugged her earlier all nod along while she speaks.

Liv hands out empty journals to the newcomers before sitting in an empty chair. She glances at Collin in the back and then asks one of the older men if he'd like to share a passage of his writing. In a thick Scottish accent, the man begins describing a piece he wrote inspired by losing his wife of 50 years.

Back in Boston, she'd assisted her faculty advisor with these community classes as part of her fellowship. When she came to Aberdeen, her new advisor encouraged her to start it up here, if for no other reason then for her thesis. Collin had been witness to the early planning and hand-wringing that went into getting this group together. He's thankful to be able to see her doing what she loves. He's glad she's even found something she loves.

After pairing up discussion partners, Liv walks around the outer edges and comes to him, resting a hand on his back. "Almost done, I promise."

Instinctively, he takes her hand and weaves his fingers into hers. "Take your time," he says. "I'm just here to learn."

She grins and plays with his fingers. "Let's go eat at that pub down the street after this." She squeezes his hand and he releases her, following her with his gaze as she rejoins the group.

When the workshop is finished, Collin helps her clean up before they leave. "Ready for that drink?" He loops her arm through his. "And fish and chips?"

She nods, staring at her feet.

"Hey," he says before they cross the street. "That girl that came in the beginning and then left – what was that all about?"

Liv tenses.

"You seemed upset. Is everything okay?"

She unlinks her arm and puts her hands in the pockets of her coat. "Not really," she says. "There are two high school girls that come to the group. I think I told you about them before... Bailey and Sam?"

He nods even though she won't look at him. "Yeah, I remember." A knot settles into his stomach. Those two girls were her earliest participants last year, apparently hearing about the group from a teacher. One of them – he can't remember which – has leukemia.

Liv sighs. "Well, tonight, that was Bailey. Apparently, Sam passed away a couple of days ago and she wanted me to know."

He stops walking. "God, I'm so sorry."

She glances up at him for only a moment and he can see her glossy eyes in the light of the crosswalk.

"Are you okay?" He reaches for her hand, but she takes a small step back.

"Yeah, I'm fine. Let's go." She waves for him to follow her across the street.

Once they're seated in a corner booth of the pub, she remains quiet, only giving a small nod as he asks about plans for the next day. He wants to get her out of her own head, but she's already shut down.

The last time she'd been like this was when they spent time together here on New Years' instead of at the cemetery in Boston. She'd known she wouldn't be able to go back during the break for weeks, but she still shut him out the entire weekend.

"Are you seeing other people when we're not together?" she finally asks, her eyes focused on her mug of lager.

"No," he answers without hesitation. "Are you?"

"Yes."

He watches her. "No, you're not."

"Not right now," she says. "But I will. And you should too."

He settles into his seat. "Where is this coming from?"

She shrugs. "I mean, we're keeping things casual, right? I told you from the beginning I don't want anything serious."

He fights the tightness growing in his chest.

"I want us to stay like this," she says, only now meeting his gaze. "Nothing more. I want to see other people too."

The words prick him with their sharpness. This feels like a test of some kind, but a test of what? Does she really want to see other people? He doesn't. More importantly, can he really share her? "Okay. Whatever you want."

Chapter 37

She couldn't sleep last night.

The fear that she'd managed to corner in her mind crossed the line when she heard about Sam. She knew Sam - beautiful Sam - was sick, but the loss still shocked her. Sam dragged Bailey to the group the first few times because she knew what was coming and was worried her best friend couldn't accept it. The writings she shared privately with Liv all expressed peace about her illness and inevitable death. Most of her essays were about her hopes for Bailey and her family once she passed.

Liv had allowed herself to feel secure these past few months with Collin. Sam's passing was a reminder of how quickly all of this could go away.

Collin shifts on the bed, turning to face her. "Are you awake?" He stifles a yawn and reaches out to brush a strand of hair from her forehead.

"Yeah," she says softly. When they'd returned from the pub last night, they sat on her bed and watched TV in silence before he kissed her and fell asleep. "Want to grab some coffee?"

Collin is deep in thought on their walk to the coffee shop down the street, only opening his mouth when they sit at a table by the window. "I don't want to see other people," he says, staring out at the misty view of the sea.

She swallows a mouthful of latte and sets down her mug. "What?"

He looks at her. "I don't want to be with anyone else. I want to be with you. Just you." His eyes are so clear in this moment, so expressive.

She glances down at the watermark forming under her mug. "Collin-"

"I've wanted that for a long time now."

She shakes her head.

"What do you want, Liv? Do you really want to date someone else?"

She sighs. She actually has no desire to be with someone else. She knows that she could easily only ever have Collin in her bed again. That's what she wants. "No. I want *you* to date someone else." More than her own selfish desire to be with him, she wants him to be happy, to be okay if - when - something happens to her. She wants him to find a woman who doesn't have this invisible clock counting down to the inevitable.

"What the hell does that mean?"

She leans forward, resting her arms in front of her. "I know this isn't enough for you," she says in a low voice, avoiding his eyes.

"Why isn't this enough for me?" He wraps his hand around hers.

"I don't want a family."

"Okay. And?"

Her cheeks grow warm. "And you do."

"I have Mila," he says. "I don't need any more kids."

"But you want more." She pauses and glances at her hands. "And I don't even want to get married."

"Maybe I don't want to either."

She narrows her eyes. "You don't want to *ever* get married?"

He shrugs. "I'm completely neutral on the issue."

"Collin, I'm not going to be responsible for you settling."

"You're right," he says. "You're not responsible. It's my decision. And I'm not settling. I just know that I want to be with you."

She frowns. "I don't know if I want to be with you - or anyone - forever."

"I know. I didn't mean forever. I want to be with you right now. And for whatever amount of time you want to be with me."

She holds his gaze, melting into the heat of his hand on hers. "Okay, then."

* * *

Collin's unsure how to read her the remainder of Saturday morning. She's quiet as they walk back to her apartment after coffee. He keeps his distance from her when they arrive until she follows him into her room and leads him to the bed. His confusion grows with each passionate kiss and each shuddering sigh.

They lay in silence after, his arm around her shoulders, her eyes lifted to the ceiling.

"I love you." He stares at her, his eyes tracing her face. "I have for a long time."

She raises her head from the pillow, supporting herself on one arm. "What?"

"I love you."

She sits up completely and turns to face him. "Why would

227

you say that? Why now?"

"Jesus Christ, Liv." He repositions himself on the bed. "I didn't think that was new information," he says. "I think I've made it pretty obvious how I feel about you."

She shakes her head. "I just told you I don't want anything serious," she sets her jaw.

"I know," he says. "And I told you I'm fine with that. We don't have to put a label on us, but I'm not to act like I don't feel this way about you." The sinking feeling in the pit of his stomach protests. Maybe he's not fine with it. "Come on. You know I love you." He wonders if this sounds desperate. Maybe it is. It doesn't matter, though. This is how he feels. He needs her to know, even if it changes everything. Or changes nothing.

She puts a hand to her face. "Why can't you leave this alone?"

He sits up, his body rigid. "I don't know what's gotten into you," he says. "You have to help me out here...what's going on? Do you not want to be with me? Is that what this is all about?"

She looks down at the blankets. "No."

"Then, why are you pushing me away?"

"I'm not," she sighs. "I just want us to be on the same page. That's all."

"How do you feel about me, Liv?"

She grips the sheets in her fists. "You're my best friend."

His stomach tightens and the air leaves his lungs, as if she's taken a sledgehammer to his chest. He feels everything shatter within him. "That's it?" he manages. "What about Logan and Adam?"

She winces.

"You could date them, but we're what? Friends with benefits? You want to go on like this forever?"

"No," she protests. "It was different with them. They weren't...you're different, okay?"

"Liv-"

She turns away. "What do you want from me?"

"Nothing," he says in defeat. He only now realizes that's what he can expect from her. Nothing. "Maybe I should go back home." He can't stay here any longer.

She still won't look at him. "Okay." She pulls on her clothes and leaves the room, closing the door behind her.

He sits for a second before grabbing his phone and searching for an earlier flight.

Liv is curled up on the sofa, staring out the window at the park when he comes out with his bag.

"I'm on standby for the 4 o'clock flight," he says. He'll have to spend the rest of the afternoon in the airport, but there's time for her to stop him. He wishes she would.

She stands up, looking at the bag in his hand. She opens her mouth as if to say something, but then shuts it.

"Let's maybe talk in a few days, okay?"

She nods. "Yeah."

He wants to kiss her one last time, but he has a feeling she might pull away. And that would only make this so much worse. "Okay...bye." He turns and opens the door.

"Collin, I-" Her voice is so soft, he almost doesn't hear it.

He looks at her and she holds his gaze, her blue eyes as clear as crystal.

"Um, text me when you get home, okay?"

That's it? He sighs. "Okay. I will."

Chapter 38

There's nothing Liv hates more than a funeral.

One of her earliest memories—so faint that she's sometimes wondered if it was a memory of a dream—is of attending her parents' funeral when she was a baby.

She remembers the warped faces of her grandfather and Ella as they tried to hold back tears, the loud, haunting melodies of the hymns sang by a small choir.

Sam's funeral isn't like that.

When Liv finally works up the nerve to push past the door into the foreboding church, she sees Bailey and other high school girls dressed in yellow as they arrange photos on a bulletin board. Bailey spots Liv and comes over, her eyes and nose raw and red.

"Are you okay?" Liv asks as the girl embraces her.

Bailey nods, releasing Liv and pushing back a strand of blonde hair. "Me and the girls are making a collage," she sniffles. "We want Sam's parents to have it." She takes Liv's hand and brings her to the group of girls. They all awkwardly glance at her and then turn back to their task. Other attendees stiffly move around them on the way to the sanctuary.

Liv looks through the photos on the board, feeling everything break within her at the sight of Sam. Seeing Sam's smile and her bright eyes makes it feel impossible that someone so lively could now be gone. In most of the pictures, Sam is wearing yellow. Now that she thinks about it, she's only ever seen Sam in various shades of yellow. She suddenly feels drab and dim in her all-black clothing.

"Yellow was her favorite color?" she asks.

Bailey nods. "Yeah, we're wearing it for her today."

Liv can barely look Sam's parents in the eyes when Bailey introduces them before the service. Her father appears stunned, his gaze going right through Liv and everyone else in the room. Her mother is more composed and thanks Liv for her kindness to her daughter, tearing up when Bailey walks away.

"I hope she can handle this," Sam's mother says, squeezing Liv's hand. "Bailey was Sammy's best mate. She's going to be so lost without her. But I think you've helped her find a little peace."

Despite her kind words, Liv feels worthless as she enters the sanctuary, keeping a distance from the open casket up front. Has Liv squandered her life by living under a shadow? What would Sam have made out of the same time Liv's been granted?

During the memorial service, she wonders if Sam's parents are angry. She is. She's been angry her whole life but never able to focus that energy at any one person. She's angry that life can be so short and angrier that death exists at all.

She returns to her apartment an hour later, drained and tipsy from the toast in Sam's honor. She collapses onto the bed, holding her phone up to her face. Since Collin left early last Saturday, they've exchanged infrequent and terse texts, but haven't spoken.

She reflects back on what Sam's mother said about how Liv had helped Bailey find peace. How could this be when she's never found it herself? For all her talk about writing to cope, she's not sure she's ever actually healed from the tragedies of her past.

How were Sam's parents able to carry on all these years, knowing that their only child wouldn't survive her youth?

Maybe they found some comfort in knowing in advance. For Liv, when she learned of Ella's diagnosis, only fear and anger rooted deeper inside her. That anxiety of waiting for the end rattled her in a different way than how her grandfather's unexpected death had.

How does everyone else live without this constant pall? After all, no one is guaranteed any amount of time in this world. How does everyone else move past the fear and uncertainty of death to actually live?

Liv presses her palms against her eyes as the tears she's been holding in for days make their escape. It doesn't matter how everyone else does it, she decides. Can she?

Chapter 39

Her fingers dig into vinyl armrests. She manages to focus her gaze out the window, down at the North Sea as the sun sets behind it. She opened the blind nearly half an hour ago, but only now, as the plane seems steady, can she attempt to look.

She almost left the airport without boarding several times. Her memories of the flight last year from Boston and the turbulence made her wither and then walk to the back of the line. Thinking about Collin made it both worse and better.

As she thinks of him now, of how they left things, she closes her eyes again. She realizes what she's truly afraid of.

To die like this. To die as nothing to anyone. To die alone. To die before she's created anything to leave behind. This is her greatest fear.

She opens her eyes again and watches the shadow of the plane on the clouds, her heart pounding in her chest.

For her, love had always been one-sided. It was a lasting ache that burned within her forever after everyone was gone. She feels that ache when she thinks about Collin, but it's hotter, lighting a part of her heart that's different from where she held the family she's lost. And it isn't one-sided. He's still here. Still breathing air and filling space on the planet above ground. Although she doesn't know for how long.

That's what scares her the most about her love for Collin. The very idea of leaving him alone on earth, unable to walk beside him or speak to him hurts like a knife in her chest that threatens to kill every soul she carries there. The idea of losing him hurts even more. And if he left, the fire inside her, the one keeping her alive, will go out too.

The look in his eyes the last time she saw him haunted her all week. She broke his heart. Of course he loves her. She loves him too.

That's why she's enduring this tortured plane ride. That's why she missed all her classes today to pack up and figure out how to get to him.

Chapter 40

When the doorbell rings, he's so certain it's his Chinese food delivery that he opens the door without checking the peephole.

"Hi."

His mouth snaps closed in astonishment. He stares into Liv's eyes for a moment, collecting himself. "Hi."

She only has an over-the-shoulder bag on her, her clothes and hair are soaking wet. The weather is precisely the reason he decided to order takeout tonight.

"Do you want to come in?"

She nods and he opens the door wider, setting his wallet back on the hallway table. It isn't until he closes the door that the real question dawns on him. "How did you—did you fly here?"

She pushes back the wet strands of hair from her forehead. "Yeah." She glances around the apartment. "I'm sorry. I should've called."

"It's okay." He still can't believe she's suddenly here standing in front of him. In the week since he left Aberdeen, he's been in a daze. He successfully dodged his coworkers' questions about why he wasn't taking a few days off anymore like planned.

Liv knots and wrings her hands. "I..." she sighs. "Collin, I..." Her lips purse. She takes a big breath. "I..." Her cheeks fill and she spins, clutching the hall table and doubling over, vomiting onto the wood floors before falling to her knees.

Collin slides down beside her, holding her hair back over her shoulders as she continues to wretch. He tries to breathe through his mouth.

Her body goes limp and she rests her head against his shoulder. "I'm sorry," she slurs.

It's only now that the smell of alcohol reaches him. "How much did you drink?" He wraps his arm around her waist and gently raises her to her feet.

She groans and wipes her mouth. "Four...ten?"

"Jesus. Fourteen?" Should he take her to the hospital?

She shakes her head as he sets her on the edge of his bed, her clothes creating a puddle onto the sheets. "Ten."

Still. "When? How long ago?"

She slumps onto the bed. She holds up two fingers. "Three at the gate," she says. "Four on the plane." She gestures vaguely toward the bedroom door. "Three over there."

He sighs. "You stopped by a pub?"

She turns and faces him, tugging at her bag and coat.

He helps her untangle both and she tosses them to the floor. "Are you going to be sick again?"

She moves her head onto his lap. "I think I'm okay." She closes her eyes.

Collin brushes her hair away from her face. "Why did you come all this way?"

"I wanted to tell you something," she says softly.

He's awake for the first time in a week. He's not sure if it's from the reeking smell permeating throughout the apartment or that Liv is beside him again. He chooses to believe the latter. "What?"

She jolts. "What?"

He laughs. "What did you want to tell me?"

She opens her eyes and stares up at him. "I love you too."

Chapter 41

A tiny, girlish voice carries through the door to Liv. There's a slight scuffle and then the sound of small footsteps retreating.

"No, not that way," Collin whispers.

Liv dares to open her eyes. They're no longer at the door, but she pulls the blanket up to her neck.

A voice so dainty and light it can only be Mila's babbles nearby.

Liv turns on her side and closes her eyelids before drifting again. When she wakes she's unsure of how much time has passed, but the sun beats through the skylight down on her, heating her body under the thick sheets.

She sits up and swings her legs over the side of the bed, tugging on her jeans and sweater from her night before. The night before. The events of the night are stored in her mind in fragments. She recalls sitting for about an hour at the pub across the street, screwing up the nerve to actually do what she came here for. From there it's spotty. She can see Collin sitting over her, stroking her hair. Her mouth tastes foul.

She stumbles out into the living room and two giant blue eyes peer up at her from the coffee table.

Mila has several stuffed animals laid out in front of her, her small pudgy hands around a baby rattle. She evaluates Liv from top to bottom with a tentative smile.

Liv takes a half step back toward the bedroom. "Oh. Hi. Are you Mila?"

The baby blinks at her, her blonde ringlets bouncing by her cheeks. Mila sits back on her legs, releasing her grip on her toy.

Liv doesn't move. "I'm Liv."

"Pa!"

Pa? The sound of running water in the kitchen suddenly stops and after the patter of hasty footsteps, Collin appears around the corner. Eyes wide, almost as big as his daughter's, he regards Liv. "Hey," he says. "Good morning." He glances down at Mila and scoops her up. "I'm going to give her something to drink real quick. Come sit down."

Mila continues staring at Liv as they enter the kitchen.

"Here you go," he says, setting Mila into a high chair at the counter. "I'll be right back." He closes the door to the kitchen and walks to Liv. "Sorry, I didn't realize you woke up already."

She shakes her head. "It's fine."

He casts a glance at the kitchen. "I know this is awkward, but Evi dropped off Mila this morning. She's going to be with me the next couple of days."

She shrugs. "Yeah, of course."

"Are you hungry?"

Her eyes focus on the front door behind him, but she resists the impulse to bolt. "Yes."

* * *

Liv doesn't relax the entire time she's at the table with him and Mila. He notices that Liv actually grows smaller and wilts in her chair the more that Mila pays attention to her.

Mila pulls herself up in the living room, toddling a few steps toward Liv before falling to the ground and crawling the rest of the way.

Liv swallows her coffee. "Look at you," she says awkwardly patting Mila's head.

Mila reaches her arms up to Liv and panic fills her eyes as she glances at Collin.

"She wants you to pick her up," he says.

She nods and avoids Mila's sharp gaze. "What if I drop her?" She takes in a deep breath.

"You'll be fine."

Liv nods again, sliding her hands under Mila's arms and picking her up. "She's heavier than I thought." Mila snuggles into Liv's chest, gently grasping a handful of her long dark hair in her tiny fist.

Collin joins Liv on the sofa and tousles Mila's hair. It's like the softest yarn under his fingers. "Yeah, she gets bigger by the month. That's kind of how babies work."

Mila wriggles from Liv's arms and crawls onto Collin's lap.

"She's not going to bite you, you know?" Collin says, cradling Mila.

Liv smiles. "I know. I'm just not...good with kids."

She's never really given it a chance. Every time she's been to his family's house for Christmas, she's kept a distance from Beth and James's children. He sets the dishes in the sink with a light clang. "She likes you, so you're in. Relax a little."

She sighs.

"I'm taking Mila to a local flower market and then to the park today." He pauses, trying to detect any emotion from Liv's expression. "Do you want to come?"

At the mention of the park, Mila's eyes brighten and she lifts her arms above her head, almost hitting Collin's chin. Mila prefers sunlight whenever she can get it, growing toward cloudless skies like a blooming flower. She thrives in the hottest days in Amsterdam, which are never as hot as they can get in Boston. Even Collin doesn't really mind summer here.

He laughs. "I was thinking we could picnic maybe."

Mila emits a little squeal and squeezes Liv's thumb.

Liv cracks, her lips parting into a grin. "Okay, sure."

Chapter 42

She tries to catch a moment to ask Collin about last night, but guilt overwhelms her every time she opens her mouth. After all she said and did last time, she's crashed into his life unannounced, intruding on his weekend with his daughter.

She watches from afar as he holds Mila's hand while she toddles beside him at the floating flower market, letting her pick from as many different vendor stalls as she wants. She follows behind them like a shadow, unable to parse the emotions that well up in her when she watches Mila slip her tiny fingers into Collin's hand.

Joy? Regret? Jealousy? If so, then jealousy of what?

That Mila will grow up knowing her incredible father or that Liv will never be the one to share this tiny, fair-haired fae of a child with him? Maybe neither. Maybe she's jealous of the ease with which Mila possesses herself and her surroundings, the ease with which she maneuvers through the world even only after living in it for a few months.

Collin hands Mila a bundle of flowers and whispers to her. She shyly glances back at Liv before tottering a couple of steps to Liv and pushes the bouquet of green chrysanthemums. She smiles at Liv, her hands trembling slightly under the weight of the flowers.

"Thank you." No sooner does Liv accept the gift than Mila grabs Collin's hand again.

He smiles at Liv and gestures for her to come closer. He folds her back into their tiny herd when choosing a packed picnic basket at the market.

It isn't until they arrive at the park that she's alone with him. Mila eagerly devoured her small portion of food so she could turn and clap toward the geese by the pond.

Collin looks at Liv. "Are you okay?"

She sips from her bottle of sparkling water. "I think so," she says. "What happened last night?" By now, she's figured out she threw up. She recalls bending over and unloading all over Collin's foyer with a shudder.

"You don't remember?" He casts a glance at Mila.

Liv rubs her head, pushing her sunglasses further up the bridge of her nose. "No, but I feel like I owe you an apology."

"For what?"

She stares out at the water. "I don't know. For what I said last time, for starters."

He meets her eyes. "It's fine. I know you didn't mean it."

"How?"

He smiles. "You told me last night."

Oh god. What else did she say in her drunken state? "I said I was sorry?"

"No," he says. "Not in so many words."

She can tell he's toying with her.

"Why did you come here?"

She picks at the tops of the shoelaces on her sneakers. It's so hard to say. Does everyone have as hard a time getting these words out? She recognizes only now that their relationship has devolved into a series of push and pulls. Her love for him and her fragile dependence on his love for her fill her with hope and dread. So, she pushes him away. Then, the picture of what her life looks like without him and without that type of love frightens her more and she pulls him back in.

She surveys him as he leans back with his hands on their small picnic blanket, his legs stretched before him, watching Mila bounce on the picnic blanket as a duck waddles past. His hair is lighter than when they first met. The change was subtle, but she'd noticed the sunstreaks the first time she visited him in Amsterdam after the permanent move. She imagines, only for a moment, that she can let him go. That she can release both of them from this sick game she's playing. She'd be miserable and she could stay that way alone, without dragging him down with her. Seeing him now is like looking through a window, peering in at what his normal life looks like without her. He's happy.

Collin turns to her when she doesn't respond.

"I don't know," she says finally. She crosses her legs and sets her bottle on the nearby grass. She does know. She knows what she came here to say, but the words are lodged within her throat. She swallows.

Mila leaps onto the blanket, bounding into Collin's arms and giggling.

* * *

"She's a great kid." Liv wraps her hoodie tighter around her chest and nestles into the sofa. She'd almost fallen asleep listening to Collin's voice reading aloud in the room down the hall.

He leans his head against the doorway to the living room.

"Yeah, she is." He smiles, a sleepy but content expression. Mila didn't nap, she chattered at the two of them with a nervous energy the rest of the day until her eyes began to droop. "Do you want some tea?" He takes a step toward the kitchen.

"Collin, wait." Her feelings have been building more and trying to claw their way out throughout the day. It's only now that her hangover has finally subsided and she's able to think clearly.

He stops.

"Sit down, please," she says. "I need to say something."

He lowers onto the cushion beside her.

She makes the mistake of reading his eyes and quickly looks away. "This must be...confusing." She runs a hand through her hair. "I mean, after last time, it must be weird for you that I just showed up like this."

He shrugs. She detects a wry tug of his lips. "I get it," he says.

"Good. Then explain it to me." For all the introspection she's done in the past days, she still feels lost sitting next to him. She wonders if she'll ever make sense of them together.

There's no doubt about it now. He's smiling. It's subtle, but she can see it. "Clearly," he begins. "Despite all the shit you say to me, you still find me irresistible."

Relief eases the tightness in her shoulders and she laughs. "Maybe it is just that simple."

He nods slowly. "I think maybe it is."

She leans her head onto his shoulder. "I do say a lot of shit, don't I?"

"Constantly." His voice lowers.

She kisses him, something like hunger settling into her gut when their lips meet. No matter how many times they touch, that sensation remains the same.

He returns her fervor and more, placing a hand behind her head and deepening the embrace. He tastes different, sweeter from the wine at their picnic.

When they part, her fingers are still laced behind his neck. "I didn't mean a single thing I said last time. I'm sorry," she breathes.

"I know."

Does he really know what she was so terrified of before? She tugs on him. "Help me out. You could at least pretend to deny it."

He laughs. "You told me yourself last night."

Her eyes widen. "Okay, what did I say?"

He wraps a lock of her hair around his thumb. "You said you love me."

She fights the urge to pull away. The intensity in his eyes makes her entire body weak. "Oh."

"Do you, Liv? Is that why you came here?"

"Yes." She bites her lip. "I don't know why it's so hard to say."

His smile widens.

"I don't know why I'm like this."

He lowers his arms around her waist and hugs her into him.

She presses her cheek against his warm shoulder. "I think I'm scared."

He doesn't say anything.

"I'm scared to be happy with you."

He kisses her again, longer this time. "Why?" he whispers against her hair.

She sighs and leans deeper into his arms. "I can't lose you too." For a moment she wonders if he can understand exactly what she means. She has her answer when he clings to her more desperately.

"You won't."

Chapter 43

FIVE MONTHS LATER

"I think it's pretty clear you've made the right choice." Collin glances at Liv before setting her gigantic suitcase on the carpet.

"Oh?" she asks. "And why is that?"

He surveys the various bags strewn around his room. *Our* room, he corrects himself. "University of Amsterdam is the Harvard of Europe."

Liv laughs, taking out a small stack of folded shirts from a bag beside the closet. "I'm pretty sure that's Oxford."

"Okay. Then UvA is the Oxford of the Netherlands."

She nods approvingly. "Okay, sure."

He pauses after setting another one of her bags on the floor. After another eight months of living apart, he loves seeing her here. He can picture waking up every morning beside her. No oceans or seas or any other bodies of water between them. He walks up behind her and wraps his arms around her waist.

"What?" She glances at him.

"I'm so happy you're here."

She leans back against him. "Me too." She sighs. "But this is going to be different for us, isn't it?"

"What do you mean?"

She turns around to face him. "What if we don't like each other if we can't escape?" Her lips shadow a smile, but her eyes betray genuine concern.

He squeezes her once more before letting her go. "There's always an escape." He gestures out the window. "The pub's right across the street."

She lets out a surprised laugh.

"That's where I'm going when I get sick of you," he teases.

"What about when we're angry at the same time? Do I need to find my own spot?"

He shrugs. "Or just sit at the other end of the bar."

She nods. "Sounds like a plan."

Their first night of officially living together ends in a quiet collapse under the sheets with a pile of Liv's stuff at the foot of the bed. "How do you feel about this?" She tugs at the neckline of her oversized t-shirt and rolls onto her side to face him.

"You mean, am I already tired of living with you?" He winds his arm around her. "You've only been here for a few hours."

"I know," she says. "But it's a little weird, right? Every time we've, you know, *been* together, we always knew one of us would have to leave eventually."

"Yeah, that's what makes this so much better. We can finally settle in and relax instead of only having a few weeks at a time together." He wonders if there's a different reason for her wariness. "Are you sure you're okay with getting your Ph.D. here?"

Her eyes flicker, but she holds his gaze. "Of course. I heard it's the Oxford of the Netherlands."

He sighs. "We could've figured this out if you really wanted to go to Harvard." Or Brown. Or Oxford. Or Cambridge. Or any of the other prestigious schools she'd been accepted into.

"I know. I wanted to go here, though." She's such a terrible liar.

"It's not too late, you know," he says. "You can still go wherever you want."

She lightly taps his chest. "Nice try. I knew you were already sick of me."

"No, I just-"

She kisses him before settling back onto her pillow. "I know, but I'm sticking around. There's nothing left in Boston for me." She ended up selling her family's house there only a few months ago after taking out loans to pay off the property tax that continued to accrue in her absence. Now, her ties to the city are limited to the lone, cheap storage unit holding her entire family's history. And with the money from the sale, she can afford to go to school and take whatever low-paying fellowship she wants for the next four years. Collin had insisted that he would support her anyway, but she was equally insistent on pitching in for rent.

He can feel the weight of this sacrifice that she's made. It's nothing like the sacrifice he would've had to make - to leave behind seeing Mila every week - but he knows Liv had dreamed of finishing her studies at Harvard and immediately picking up a teaching position there after graduation. University of Amsterdam hadn't even been a remote option in her mind and he's sure she wouldn't have considered going there unless they'd become serious. He never asked her to stay in Europe, but he also never offered to go with her back to the U.S. or move to Britain. She didn't tell him when she had her interview at UvA. He only found out about it when she appeared at his apartment afterward to share the good news. He wanted to say something in that moment, to tell her not to change her plans, but he couldn't muster the words. He was happy, truly happy, that they could start a real life together in the same city and in the same home.

He hugs her into his chest and kisses her dark curls. He hopes he's worth it.

Chapter 44

She's found that Amsterdam is her favorite place to run. Since cutting back on alcohol, she's actually been able to roll out of bed before Collin to go running. She doesn't listen to music here when she jogs through the labyrinth of cobblestone and pavement along the canal. Instead, she listens for the metallic roll of bicycles tires behind her and the gentle lapping of water against houseboats below in the early morning.

Liv winds around the corner of the market near their apartment before slowing her steps. She pauses on the sidewalk, resting her hands against her waist and steadies her breath, peering in through the window of the coffee shop. She takes one last deep breath and walks inside, placing her usual order, this time in the halting and flimsy Dutch she's heard Mila and Collin use. "Mag ik twee koffie?"

The boy behind the counter grins. Instead of speaking English to her like he usually does, he asks "Gewone koffie?"

She doesn't know, but she nods instead of admitting defeat.

"That's 'regular coffee,'" he says, handing her the receipt before turning his back to the machine.

She accepts the to-go cups with a quick thank you and crosses the street into the apartment lobby. When she lets herself in, Collin is frantically buttoning his striped collared shirt and sliding on his red wing shoes.

He sees her and steps out of the bedroom. "Coffee! Thank god!" He accepts one of the cups with a smile. "Why didn't you wake me up before you left?" He takes a sip and glances at the clock in the kitchen.

She sits down at the table, her sweatshirt clinging to her back. "I did," she says. "You sat up and looked at me when I told you to wake up."

He laughs. "Oh, I guess I went back to sleep after that. Anyway, I'm late. *Very* late." He bends down and kisses her before grabbing his coat and pulling it over his arms. "I'm picking up Mila after work tonight."

"Okay. Oh, coffee!"

He follows her gaze to his cup resting on the table and grabs it before turning the doorknob. "Thanks. See you tonight!" He pauses to look at her before closing the door behind him.

She clears something in her throat. She forgot Mila was coming over tonight. If she showers now, she'll still have time to get a pot roast started in the slow cooker before she has to be on campus.

She swallows another mouthful of coffee before abandoning her cup and rushing to the bathroom, shedding her sweaty clothes on the floor and stepping into the shower.

In the beginning, she'd been uncertain about how she would feel seeing Collin every day, but even more tentative about the prospect of interacting with Mila more frequently. To her surprise, she looks forward to having Mila around.

She leans against the tile as something thick catches in her throat again. As she continues to cough, a bitter iron taste coats her tongue. She bends over and coughs, only making the rattling sound harsher. Small flecks of red appear under her and swirl around the drain before disappearing. Her heart clenches. She spits into the drain and more blood splatters onto the white tile.

* * *

"Livvy?"

Liv snaps from her thoughts to see Mila's eyes peering up at her, her fingers curled around the spine of a picture book. "Hmm?"

Mila extends the book and lays it on Liv's lap. "Read me?"

She glances at the cover. "I can't, Mila. This is in Dutch." She peers into the kitchen where Collin's back is to her as he washes dishes with the water running. "Can you pick a different one?"

Mila sticks out her lower lip and scuttles across the living room to the bookshelf beside the TV.

Liv continues to stare at Collin's back. She's wanted to talk to him alone since this morning, but couldn't even bring herself to meet his gaze during dinner. She knew her eyes would betray her fear. She stumbles through a lifeless reading of the English book Mila retrieves. She can sense Mila's disappointment, but it's all she can do right now to keep breathing evenly.

It could be many benign things, the doctor had said. *But given your family history, I think it's a good idea to run some tests. Just to be sure.*

These words repeat in her mind as she listens to Collin brushing his teeth in the next room later that night. Yes. Just to be sure. Her chest tightens as if she's back in the x-ray machine.

The bathroom light flickers off. "Hey," Collin slides under the blankets beside her. "Is everything all right?"

She doesn't look at him, even in the dark. "Yeah," she says. She can only now hear the subtle hoarseness in her voice. Ella's voice had grown harsher like that before they found out. "I'm just tired." The bed squeaks lightly as Collin shifts on the mattress.

"Mila asked about you. She thought maybe you were sick or something. Are you feeling okay?"

No, she's not okay. She swallows, a metallic taste still in her throat from earlier. It's cruel how quickly this attempted life she's building with Collin could disappear. "I'm fine." She can feel his stare. "I forgot she was coming over tonight."

He's silent for a moment. "I thought I told you this morning."

She sighs. "You did. But before that, I just forgot."

"Are you upset that she's here?" The shift in his tone appears suddenly.

She clenches her jaw. "No, but she requires a lot of attention." As soon as the words leave, she knows it's too late to stop the path of this conversation.

As usual, Collin's not easy to provoke. "If you need a break, maybe I can take her out alone tomorrow. You can stay here."

She closes her eyes, too aware of the heaviness in her lungs as she takes a deep breath. "I mean, I told you I didn't want a family." *No. Stop. Stop talking.* "But it's like I still have to deal with a kid that's not even mine."

Even though he's inches away from her, she can feel Collin's body tense. "It's not like it was a surprise, Liv," he says, his tone rough but measured, deliberate. "You knew she had to be a part of our life together."

"Yeah, and you knew I didn't want any children. This can't be a surprise to you either, right?"

"What's wrong with you today?" he snaps.

She tosses the blankets off and slides her feet onto the wood floor.

"Where are you going?"

She opens the door to the living room. "I can't sleep. I'm going to watch TV for a little while."

His frustrated sigh is audible even as she closes the door behind her.

Her whole body shutters. She covers the sob that escapes through her lips with both hands as she sinks onto the sofa. She sits there alone, wiping at her tears with the sleeve of her shirt before staggering to Mila's room. The little girl is asleep amongst a bundle of blankets and stuffed animals, clutching the toy pig Liv gave her for her first birthday.

In spite of herself, Liv's grown to want this. She wants her own little girl or boy with Collin. She's never spoken this to him because her fear, that deep and lingering ache, was stronger than her desires. Now, there may not even be a point in telling him.

She rubs at her eyes again. She's spent so much time nursing this fear and now it may be too late.

Chapter 45

He resents her the entire morning, not only because of her words the previous night, but because his anger pervades his thoughts as he goes around town with Mila. Laying in bed alone, he realized everything she said was irreconcilable. There's nothing he can change to make her happier.

Then as the night progressed and she didn't return, he thought Liv might be right. Perhaps he always knew she wasn't ready for this kind of relationship. Perhaps he pushed her to be someone she never could be. She had warned him, hadn't she?

It wasn't easy to coax Mila out of the apartment without Liv, but he managed to do it without ever speaking to or looking at Liv as she quietly transitioned from the couch back to the bed before Mila caught sight of her. A sinking feeling invades his stomach all day that when he returns home Liv may not be there.

He thought he'd been able to read her these past few months. Just last week when he needed to work late one night, she asked him if she could bring Mila to the University library with her. He can still see Mila and Liv's conspiratorial smiles when he walked through the door later that night and they were sharing a bowl of ice cream.

As he treks closer to the apartment that afternoon, Mila's

small, warm hand in his, his heart grows heavier with each step. He holds his breath when he turns the key in the lock and opens the door.

"Livvy!" Mila releases his hand and springs toward Liv's perch at the kitchen table.

She smiles and embraces Mila, running the back of her hand across her eyes. Her nose is red and her eyes bloodshot. "Hey, did you have fun?" she rasps.

Mila nods and wriggles free of Liv's hold. "Why didn't you come?"

Liv glances at Collin. She looks like she's going to cry. "I'm sorry. I didn't feel well."

Mila accepts this and hugs Liv once more before skipping to the bathroom in the hall.

He's still frozen beside the door, torn between comforting Liv and his aching disappointment about what's sure to come.

She stands up, but maintains her distance from him.

He glances at the bathroom door. "Can we talk?"

She sniffs. "Collin, I didn't mean anything I said last night."

The words are familiar. Too familiar. "Yes, you did. Everything you said is true. You told me you didn't want this, but I wanted to believe that...I don't know, that we could make it work."

She shakes her head. "It's not true," she says, her voice quivering. "There's nothing I'd change about this."

"I love you. But I can't keep going through this with you, especially if it's about Mila."

"It's not about her. She's perfect. And you..." She swallows. "I'm sorry."

He runs a hand through his hair. "I think maybe we should take some time to think this through." He almost can't believe the words come out of his mouth. "Just for a little while." His heart sinks when he sees Liv's expression. He almost takes it back immediately.

Her eyes well with tears. "Okay," she chokes.

* * *

The next few days, he's only going through the motions. Living under the same roof but sleeping separately is more taxing than he'd expected. Liv stays on campus much longer than usual, only appearing after dinner to sleep in the bedroom while Collin takes the couch.

At work, he barely registers the outcome of a big lunchtime meeting. He barely remembers the details of his conversation with Evi, about her business trip to Hong Kong and how she needs him to take Mila early for the week. He doesn't know exactly how he explains Liv's absence to his daughter, even, but the look she gives him unravels his heart until he can't feel it beat any longer.

He's absent when he picks Mila up from daycare and walks with her to the park. He's so absent, in fact, that he doesn't notice Mila's hand slip from his. He sees her toddle a few steps ahead of him. She glances back at him.

First, he hears the terrible sound, the sickening thud. His body lunges forward of its own accord before his mind can process the image of the tiny body under the bumper.

Chapter 46

Collin smooths back the delicate, blonde curls from Mila's forehead, careful not to touch her bruised skin. She's so quiet and still on the large white hospital bed. The doctors warned that the medicine would make her sleepy. That combined with her agonized cries had worn her out.

Evi was hysterical when he called her initially. She wouldn't be able to get a flight from Hong Kong for another two days. By the end of the conversation, Collin managed to convince her Mila was okay and she needed to stay at work. The doctors said Mila was cleared to go home with him in a few hours once they confirmed she didn't have any internal bleeding.

He didn't elaborate on that detail to Evi. He was grateful she didn't scream and blame him. She assured him that it was the driver's fault. In truth, it happened so quickly he doesn't know in that split second who had more responsibility to prevent the accident, him or the driver who was texting.

Mila's eyes close, but her grip remains tight on his finger. Her right arm is in a cast, but her left hand is free and only mildly swollen from the impact.

"Oh my god." Liv timidly steps into the room behind him, her eyes locked on Mila.

He almost completely forgot he called Liv. He can barely

remember making the call, but it was his first. Even before Evi, his fingers fumbled over the phone and dialed Liv as he waited at the hospital. He somehow managed to stumble through a strangled and panicked voicemail.

She walks up to the bed, her hands hovering over Mila's fragile body. When she turns to him, her face is covered in tears. "Is she sleeping?" She manages in a low voice.

Mila stirs slightly at Liv's voice.

Collin brushes his fingers along the girl's small hand and nods. "Yeah, I think it's the medicine they gave her."

Liv presses her fingers against her cheek. She places her other hand on Collin's shoulder.

They stand there silently, Liv's hand trembling and his eyes blurred with tears, until Mila releases his hand and relaxes even deeper into the bed.

He wipes at his eyes and stands up, pulling Mila's blanket further over her waist to keep her warm. He gestures to Liv and they step into the hallway.

"Is she going to be okay?" Liv asks immediately, unable to look away from Mila.

He follows her gaze. "They think so," he says. "They just want to wait for some test results to make sure there's no-" he stops, sensing the burning returning to his eyes. "They're planning to release her soon."

Liv's eyes fill with new tears but she hastily brushes them away. "What happened?"

"I let go of her hand." His voice quivers. "And a car—it just came out of nowhere." He shakes his head. "I wasn't paying attention."

She grabs his hand. "These things happen. It's not your fault." She wraps her arms around him. "I should've been here from the beginning," she breathes. "I'm so sorry." She releases him, but takes his hand again.

"Thanks for coming." The words feel inadequate. He wants to wipe away everything that happened earlier between them.

She tightens her grasp. "I'm going to wait with you." She does. She sits for hours by his side, sitting vigil over Mila's mangled body. When she wakes, her eyes take in Liv and she smiles, wincing a little as her lips stretch the stitches by her nose. Liv chats with Mila about her favorite book when Collin steps out to speak with the doctor.

When they arrive back at the apartment in the early morning the next day, she offers to sit and watch Mila.

He leaves Mila's door open before joining Liv in the living room. "No, let her rest," he says. He runs a hand across his face and along his tired eyes.

She reaches out and grabs his hand, leading him to their bedroom. As they lie side by side again for the first time in a long time, she strokes his hair until he's able to relax and fall asleep.

That night, before he can leave the bed to check on Mila, Liv is already up almost once every hour, peering into Mila's room and returning, trying to slip under the covers undetected.

When she does this after her last check-in, Collin winds his arm around her waist.

"You're awake?" she asks.

"Just now," he mumbles. "Is she okay?"

"Yes, she seems fine." She rolls onto her side. "Are you?"

He shakes his head. "No. I screwed up." In more than one way. "With Mila and then...I shouldn't have said what I did to you. If I hadn't—well, I wouldn't have been so distracted when..." He takes her hand into his.

Her eyes are bright even in the dark. "You were right to be angry. I didn't mean any of it, though. I want you to know that." She lifts his hand and places his knuckles to her lips. "When I think about home, it's you and Mila. For me it's terrifying to love someone as much as I love you and her." She lets out a small breath. "But today reminded me why it's worth living with that fear. I can't imagine my life without you two."

He leans forward and kisses her, pulling her against his chest. He wishes there was a way to hold her even closer than this. She's as much a part of him as any other element of his being. When he can bring himself to let go of her, he buries his face into her sweet hair, bringing his lips close to her ear. "Liv, will you stay with me? Can you tell me that you're all in, that you'll never leave?"

* * *

When he wakes up and checks on Mila, Liv is already gone. In the early hours, he saw her outline against the window, pulling on her sweatshirt and running shoes.

He's not sure what he expected, but he's still shaken by how she collapsed in tears at his question last night. That was her answer. He finally asked too much of her.

Mila's alert, eager to hold her own piece of toast. "Where's Momma?"

He sits on the edge of her bed. The swelling in her face has reduced, although the bruises have transitioned to a nastier shade of dark blue. "She's still at work, in Hong Kong, remember?" He offers her a sippy cup of juice. "But she's going to try to leave a little early to come see you." Just then his phone begins to buzz in his pocket. As if on cue, it's Evi wanting to speak with Mila. He puts it on speakerphone on the nightstand beside Mila and leaves her to cheerily speak in Dutch with a notably relieved Evi.

Liv slips in through the door, two coffee cups in hand, one balanced in the crook of her elbow. She smiles when she sees him. "Good morning." A few strands of hair stick to her temple where the only evidence of sweat lies.

He takes a step toward her and she extends one of the coffees. "Thanks."

She puts her cup down on the table and closes the gap between them. "Collin-"

"It's fine," he says quickly, setting his cup onto the counter. "Please. Just forget about it." He's decided over and over again that he'll take whatever part of herself she'll share. That's enough for him.

Her eyes glimmer, but she looks away. "I don't want to forget about it. I'm sorry I reacted that way, I just..." She's only a few inches from him now, but it feels like miles. "Just give me some time."

Chapter 47

"I want to hear about how you're doing so far." Dr. Bakker beams at Liv across his desk.

Liv looks up from her notes. "Good," she says, drawing out the word while she thinks. Her thoughts are still in the apartment with Collin. He took the day off from work. She offered to stay with him and Mila, but he remembered the scheduled meeting with her faculty advisor that she forgot. "I'm still brainstorming topics for my dissertation."

He nods, stroking his graying beard. "Yes, of course," he says. "That will take some time. Are you having any issues with classes?"

She's noticed such a difference between Dr. Bakker and her previous faculty advisor at Aberdeen. Dr. Bakker seems more concerned about her personal well-being rather than just research. Part of her thinks this may be because she'd shared too many details about her Master's thesis on therapeutic writing, but another part wonders if it's because of the professor's advanced age. Surely, he's someone's grandfather and accustomed to comforting his own family. "No, just keeping busy. I really like all my classes." She wonders if he's misread her red, puffy eyes as a sign of a school-related woe.

His keen, gray gaze softens. "Very good. So, I know it's early on, but at this point I like to ask students to take a look forward into your academic career. It helps me figure out the best way to help you." He sips from his small black mug. "What are you hoping to get out of the next five years?"

Her mouth is suddenly dry. What does she want? Five years is long. Her heart sinks. It's also too short. Much too short. Yet, depending on what the doctor says when he calls about her test results later today, five years may be the most she can hope for. She blinks, trying to hold back the fear creeping along her spine. "I want to be a professor," she says, finally. "Here, hopefully."

"That's it?"

No. She wants to be alive in the next five years. No. There's so much more that she wants if she can have it. If she can live, truly live, she wants everything. She wants Collin. She wants Mila. She wants her own kids – with Collin. She wants to see Mila grow up and have her own life.

"Well, why here?"

Liv focuses her eyes on the professor again. "I'm sorry, what?"

"Why do you want to stay in Amsterdam? Why do you want to teach here after graduation?" Dr. Bakker's eyes crinkle with a mild smile.

She clears her throat. Maybe if she believes it's possible, she can allow herself to reach out and take it.

Chapter 48

His mood deteriorated throughout the day. Between the constant reminders of the accident all over Mila's body and the lack of sleep over the past 48 hours, he senses the edge in his tone before he hangs up with his supervisor. The question was pointless anyway, but he's sure it's not nearly as idiotic as he perceives it in the moment.

Then there's the matter of Liv and his question last night. Was it too much to ask that she commit to him?

He audibly sighs and Mila turns away from the cartoons on TV to look up at him on the couch beside her. "I'm tired," she says, her eyes heavy.

Shit. He forgot to even try to put her down for her usual nap. He glances at the clock. If she sleeps now she'll be up all night. It can't be helped. She needs to rest. He stands and lifts her up. Technically, she can still walk just fine, but he saw a slight limp when she did earlier and his heart nearly tore in half. Her body goes soft and her eyes close almost immediately once he sets her on the bed. He pulls the blankets over her, tucking them just under the collar of her sunflower pajamas.

He yawns and closes her bedroom door as Liv bursts inside the apartment. Despite his weariness, he still smiles when he sees her.

She returns the favor and crosses the room, throwing her arms around his neck.

He feels that he can melt right into her warmth and sleep standing there with her.

She pulls away to look at him, her eyes gleaming. "Yes."

He blinks. "What?"

She kisses him. "I'm all in. Forever. No matter what happens."

The warmth from her skin seeps into his. "I thought-"

She nestles her face into the curve of his neck. "I told you, I just needed time." Her lips graze his cheek. "I want this - all of this - with you."

"What changed your mind?" He almost regrets the words, as if this question will shatter the most wonderful daydream and she'll vanish from his arms.

She sighs. "I don't want to be scared anymore," she says.

He takes one of her hands and wraps his fingers into hers. "Scared of what?"

She holds his gaze. "Of life." She kisses him again, longer this time.

"We have to celebrate," he says breathlessly.

"Celebrate? I should've said this to you a long time ago."

He hugs her into his chest. "It's been worth the wait. I love you."

"I love you too." She buries her face in his shoulder.

"I think I might have a gift bottle of Scotch in here some-where," he says after a moment.

Liv laughs and releases him. "Okay, go get it. Let's cele-brate."

He walks into their bedroom, opening the closet and dig-ging for the company Christmas gift bag buried under long-abandoned luggage.

When he reenters the living room, Liv is standing with her back to him, one hand holding her phone to her ear, the other white-knuckled and clutching at the kitchen counter. "Okay," she says. "Thank you."

"Who's that?" he asks once she sets the phone onto the table, still facing away from him. He steps past her and grabs two tumblers from the cabinet, catching a glimpse of her face.

She wipes at her eyes and a faint smile appears as she leans against the granite counter.

"What's wrong?" He places everything on the table and takes her arm.

She laughs a little, pulling him closer. "Nothing. Absolutely nothing."

About the Author

Kate Allen is a lifelong bibliophile and writer, her earliest works dating back to when she was seven. Since then, her writing tools of choice have evolved from crayons to a laptop. In addition to her writing and other creative shenanigans, she practices law and spends time with her husband and their loveably goofy dog.

You can connect with me on:

🌐 http://www.kateallenauthor.com

CPSIA information can be obtained
at www.ICGtesting.com
Printed in the USA
BVHW040256230321
603180BV00005B/881